M000170075

First published 2021

The History Press
97 St George's Place, Cheltenham,
Gloucestershire, GL50 3QB
www.thehistorypress.co.uk

British Library Cataloguing in Publication Data.
A catalogue record for this book is available from the British Library.

ISBN 978 0 7509 9509 2

Typesetting and origination by Typo•glyphix, Burton-on-Trent
Printed and bound in Great Britain by TJ Books Ltd.

MIX
Paper from
responsible sources
FSC® C013056

FOLK TALES OF SONG AND DANCE

WRITTEN AND ILLUSTRATED BY

PETE CASTLE

The History Press

CONTENTS

ACKNOWLEDGEMENTS

Sue, of course, for being a friend, companion, support, wife and lover for over fifty years.

Nicky Rafferty for being the second person to read the book and for the enthusiastic response.

Taffy Thomas for 'Fill the House'.

Madge Spencer for 'The Guitar Player'.

Richard Martin for 'Bee, Harp and Bum-clock'.

Katherine Soutar for the beautiful cover.

To everyone who has supported me over the years.

To everyone at The History Press for getting the book out in a difficult time.

INTRODUCTION

When I started work on this book I thought I was simply writing a book about song and dance but I soon realised I was writing a book about sex, murder, jealousy and just about all the other 'seven deadly sins'!

I started playing guitar at about 14 or 15, not because it was a way of attracting girls – although I suppose that might have been a contributory factor, but just because I wanted to play music. I was very surprised that my parents agreed to buy me one. The guitar was very fashionable at that time but not a 'respectable' instrument. In the films of their

young days – the 1930s/40s – the guitar was often an instrument used as shorthand for a disreputable character. In many of them, particularly Westerns, the baddy was foreign, lazy, smoked a cigar and strummed a guitar. That motif carried on into the McCarthy-era 'Reds under the beds' witch-hunts of the 1950s and '60s against Communist infiltration in the entertainment industry in America. They produced leaflets on 'How to Spot a Communist' and two of the signs to look for were – they wear a beard and they play the guitar! Woody Guthrie took the opposite view with the slogan on his guitar: 'This machine kills Fascists'. I have continued to play the guitar ever since, professionally since 1978, alongside storytelling, which came a bit later.

I suspect that musicians have always laboured under a disreputable reputation. It wasn't invented for 1960s guitar players: it applied to 1860s fiddlers and 1260s harpists just as much – perhaps even to the bones players from some Stone Age culture. I have seen a musician described as 'someone you would not want your daughter to marry'. That could be simply because it has always been a very unpredictable occupation, but there is more to it than that. Sailors are supposed to have a girl in every port and some musicians do as well. Conversely, musicians have always been seen as 'glamorous' and been prey for young women who wanted a trophy. That was particularly true in the 1960s/70s when being a 'groupie' was the aim of many teenage girls. I well remember being on the bus home from school, we'd just left the bus station, and the cry went up, 'It's the Searchers!' and the bus emptied of girls at the next stop. It was the pop group The Searchers, who were playing in town that night and had gone out for a walk.

Dancing is similarly problematic. Professional dancers were often considered to be prostitutes whether they were or not. Dancing is frowned on if not banned outright by some religious groups. Even among relatively ordinary, liberal people some types of dancing are more accepted than others and the latest dance crazes always rub the older generation up the wrong way – probably deliberately!

So how do you write a book of folk tales like this? What is your aim? This is my fourth one for THP and my approach has gradually changed. With the first one – *Derbyshire Folk Tales* – I simply related the tales with nothing added, nothing taken away. You could have taken them off the page and told them. I gradually added a bit more of myself with each of the next two. This time I have used a variety of approaches. Some tales I have told straight or have just added short comments or introductions. A few though, I have allowed to move away from the simple folk tale as I would tell it. I have approached it more like a novella and included many more abstract ideas. This wasn't really pre-planned. Once I started writing, some of the stories took over and demanded that of me. I have heard 'proper authors' say this and have never really understood it before ... now I do. I hope the variety of approaches works for you.

One of my sources, T.W. Rolleston, in a rather prim 1910 book called *The High Deeds of Finn*, sums it up like this:

> My aim ... has been artistic, not scientific. I have tried, while carefully preserving the main outline of each story, to treat it exactly as the ancient bard treated his own material ... that is to say, to present it as a fresh work of poetic imagination.

In other words, these stories don't belong on the page – and definitely not in a museum – they should be out there on the tongue and in the world.

These stories came to me from here, there and everywhere – word of mouth, books, websites ... BUT I avoided the best resource of all – other books in The History Press' Folk Tales series! I wanted to avoid the versions of my contemporaries and colleagues so, even when I knew a particular teller had a version of a story in their book I made a point of not looking at it. If, therefore, you find one of my tellings is remarkably similar to yours then it is because a) we both went to the same source or b) great minds think alike!

The few stories that I have learned directly from contemporary tellers I did so with their knowledge and permission, and usually from them not their books.

So where and how did I find them? Some I have been telling or singing for many years – a few even pre-date my interest in storytelling! Some I knew of before I started writing but have never used; others I found by directed research – can I find a story about … and a few I came across by sheer chance when I was looking for something else. I have found that experience especially thrilling, particularly when it turns out to be a really good tale.

These stories cover a huge vista of space and time. They are almost all from the British Isles but that doesn't mean some of them don't feel 'foreign' to me because the British Isles includes England, Ireland, Wales, Scotland and the Northern Isles, where there is the added flavour of Viking influence and links with Scandinavia. The timescale ranges from prehistory to the present day. Of the few that I have imported from further afield, there is a Romanian tale that I use regularly and which fits alongside Glasgerion perfectly, and one from Estonia that I chanced upon and which shares themes and ideas with many others in the collection. It illustrates that people share the same stories wherever they live.

It also introduces an idea about which there has been a lot of discussion recently – cultural appropriation. I thought (or was it 'worried') about that a lot. I am quite happy reworking and re-telling English stories but when I get on to the very ancient Irish and Welsh legends that are treated by some as almost religious texts I'm not so sure. I am not an expert on the stories or the cultures. Am I misunderstanding something? Not getting the hidden meanings? I have tried to treat them as I would any other story and not allowed cultural baggage to get in the way. I hope my versions do not upset anyone.

Philip Pullman discusses that problem in an essay called 'Magic Carpets'. He says:

> Should we storytellers make sure we pass on the experience of our own culture? Yes, of course. It's one of our prime duties … But should we refrain from telling stories that originated elsewhere …? Absolutely not. A culture that never encounters any others becomes first inward-looking, and then stagnant, and then rotten.

I hope this collection does its bit towards keeping our storytelling traditions alive. You can help it by taking them, making them your own, and telling them.

Pete Castle, Belper, 2020

GLASGERION

Glasgerion was the king's chief harper. He was known throughout the land as the finest harper, singer and storyteller of his generation, and possibly of any generation, and his skill was so much above that of all the other bards that he was held in awe throughout the land. In Scotland he was known as Glenkindie and in Wales as Bardd Glas Geraint – Geraint, the Blue Bard.

When he played and sang, Glasgerion could charm the fish to leap from the sea or cause a stone to weep. When he sat in a quiet spot, the animals would gather round and lay peacefully together listening to his harp strings sing. He had musical conversations with the birds and each learned melodies from the other. In his favourite spot even the rocks had edged forwards to form a circle around his seat to hear him better. When he wanted them to, his songs could drive men to war or women to love. His stories could so entrance men that he could intervene in deadly feuds and by the time his story had ended they had forgotten what they were arguing about and went home arm in arm, the best of friends.

That was Glasgerion's life and had been for many years. He had served his apprenticeship and learned his trade. Now he was in his prime – or past it, he sometimes felt.

One evening Glasgerion was sitting in his master's hall letting his fingers play idly over the strings of his harp. Earlier he had entertained the assembled crowds with epic tales of heroes from the past, comic songs about foolish country folk, and erotic stories of love and courtship. He had finished with lively dance tunes and then slower, more languid airs until his master's guests had gradually sunk into their seats and dropped asleep with their heads on the table, or slipped out of the hall and taken to their beds either to sleep or to make love.

Now he was playing mostly for himself. Soon he would retire as well. Those who were still awake were otherwise engaged with talking or flirting, the food and drink was almost finished and the fire in the central hearth had burned down to a dull red glow.

The only person who seemed to be still awake and paying any attention to Glasgerion was his Lord's Lady. She sat, as she had for the past hour, with her eyes fixed on him drinking in every word he sang or spoke and every note he played. Glasgerion had been aware of her interest, had watched her watching him, and had not been able to prevent their eyes from meeting a few times.

At last she arose and walked quietly towards the staircase that led to her room. As she passed him she bent and whispered in his ear: 'Before the day dawns and the cocks crow you must come and share my bed.'

She slipped through the curtain and Glasgerion was left wondering whether she had really said what he thought she'd said. Was he misunderstanding? Or mishearing? He could imagine her inviting some handsome young warrior to her bed but surely, he was too old …

He'd had his chances in the past but he'd never been a great womaniser. Sometimes he was just too naïve and didn't understand the signals. He hadn't always got the message; he'd doubted whether they had meant what he heard; he'd been too unsure of himself to take them up on it, or too scared of the retribution their family might make if he was wrong or if he was found out. Once he'd meant to accept the invitation of a woman he really fancied but he'd been unable to find her room and the next day she had acted as though he had done her the most terrible insult.

So why now? Why had this glamorous, desirable woman chosen him – a grey-haired, bent old harper.

Glasgerion thought back over the songs he had sung and the stories he had told that evening. He had been good, he knew that. But then he was usually good and he knew his trade so well that even when he wasn't on top form he could make it appear that he was.

It must have been his music that had got him invited into her bed! He smiled to himself. That had been why he had chosen to become a musician in the first place! When he was a youth he and his friends thought musicians were glamorous and could have any girl they wanted. It was only when he had started on the path to becoming one that he had realised that if he wanted to succeed there was too much work involved to waste time on frivolous affairs with flighty girls.

So what had he played to work the magic on the most beautiful woman in the room? He had started the evening, as he always did, with a few light, frivolous items that were guaranteed to go down well with an audience that was still arriving and getting comfortable and were, maybe, not giving him all their attention. Then he had moved on to the big important ones, the ones that showed off his skill, and he mixed them up with a few dances. Towards the end when people started to fall asleep or leave for their beds, alone or not, he had lowered the mood again.

Glasgerion played his songs and told his stories and they worked their magic. But the evening did not end as it was supposed to with Glasgerion enjoying a night of bliss in the young Lady's arms … the story continues at the end. Meanwhile:

Adapted from Child#67 – Professor Francis James Child's The English and Scottish Popular Ballads. *See note to Glasgerion Part 2 for more info.*

Learning from the master and following Glasgerion's formula for a good set, I'll continue with two simple, well-known stories that suggest that you shouldn't leave the entertaining to the professionals. You must be ready to play your part.

'Tell a story, sing a song, show your bum or oot ye gan', as the old Scots saying goes!

SOMETHING TO TELL 'EM

A traveller arrived at a remote country inn one evening. He'd been on the road all day and he was tired. As soon as he entered, before he'd even had time to order a drink and a meal and book a room, the locals gathered round and started asking him where he'd come from and what he had to tell them.

'What's happening out there in the world?' they wanted to know.

'What news is there from the city?'

'What should we know?'

They all spoke at once and tried to get his attention but whatever they asked he just shrugged his shoulders and said, 'Nothing to tell you.'

'Well, alright, if you've no news then tell us a story, you must have heard a story.'

'No, nothing to tell you.'

'Well a joke then. Are there any good new jokes going around? We haven't heard a new one for ages.'

'Nothing to tell you.'

'How about a song? Have you heard any good ones? Do you play an instrument? Can you play us a tune?'

This went on and on with the locals trying their best to get some news or entertainment, or perhaps just conversation, from the traveller because they didn't meet strangers very often. But his only reply was always: 'Nothing to tell you.'

In the end they moved away and left him to his own devices.

When he'd eaten his meal the landlord showed him up to his room and he climbed into bed and was soon asleep.

In the middle of the night, when he was as fast asleep as you can be, he suddenly felt himself hauled out of bed, his nightshirt was pulled off and a warm, sticky liquid was poured over him. Then he heard his pillow being ripped open and he was sprinkled with feathers.

The result was that by the time he was fully awake he found himself lying on the floor, stark naked and covered with treacle and feathers. He looked around in amazement and saw the landlord standing in the corner laughing. 'You'll have something to tell 'em tomorrow night,' he said.

And so there is the moral: you should always be prepared to tell a story, sing a song, tell a joke or even do a dance, for you never know when it will come in useful.

Trad English.

SANDY / SANDRA

This is another story that shows you should always have a tale to tell, a song to sing, a joke, or something else with which you can participate in a gathering. It also tells an unusual tale about how the hero/heroine found one!

Late summer and the harvest was in. It was a time for rejoicing and relaxing before the cycle started all over again and the workers had to toil away to get the fields prepared ready to plant the seeds for next year. Before that though, there was the Harvest Supper, a highlight of the year. The Master always provided plenty of food and drink and everybody ate and drank as much as they could. It was a time for letting your hair down and, possibly, doing things you later regretted – rather like an office party today.

All afternoon the men had been preparing the barn: it had been swept and green branches and ribbons hung around the walls. Then a long table was erected down the length of the building and chairs and benches brought in. Candlesticks and lanterns were placed on the tables and hung from the beams. There was also a large barrel of beer, which was the most important thing for some of them! Meanwhile, the women had been busy cooking and laying out plates and bowls.

Then, when it was all ready, there was a hiatus while everyone went off to prepare themselves. The men washed and shaved, oiled their hair and put on their best clothes, for they were hoping to impress the women and girls. They in turn were doing each other's hair, sharing bits of make-up and seeing whether they could still fit into last year's dresses and swapping with each other if they couldn't. They were as eager to impress as the men were and the unmarried ones had the same hopes as the men, although perhaps not quite so openly! A tumble in the hay at the end of the evening was almost part of the ceremony and there were always a few women who found themselves 'in trouble' in the weeks afterwards.

At last the time came and everyone made their way to the barn and took their seats. There was a recognised but unspoken seating plan – the Master and Mistress were at the top of the table, the farm manager had pride of place at the foot, and the workers sat down the sides with the most senior at the head and the youngest at the foot where the manager could keep them in order.

Before anyone took their place though, the 'mow' – the Harvest Queen – made from the last sheaf and dressed to look like a woman with a crown of flowers on her head, was ceremonially carried in and seated on a throne-like chair to preside over the event.

Then grace was said and before the food was served the Master threw a purse of coins on to the table and announced that it would go to the person who could tell the best story, sing the best song, or otherwise entertain the guests in the most enjoyable way.

'Eat first,' he said, 'and while you're eating you can be planning what you are going to do. And it's no good saying you can't do anything because everyone has to take part. If you're not going to do something then leave now, before you've eaten.'

Most of the crowd had already decided on their party piece, of course, because this happened every year. It was tradition that the farm manager always sang 'To Be a Farmer's Boy', and three or four of the milkmaids got together and sang a hymn. Everyone else managed to do something but some of the younger ones were taken by surprise and didn't know what to do at first.

One of these was young Sandy. It was his first experience of this and the idea terrified him. He was a big lad but very shy and innocent. He never said very much and only spoke when he was spoken to. The idea of standing up in front of all these people who he had to work with every day and trying to tell them a story was beyond him. He didn't quite burst into tears but he stood up, red in the face, and stuttered, 'Sir, I can't do it. I haven't anything to do. I don't sing and I don't know any stories.'

'Then you can leave now,' said the Master. 'Go on, get out and don't come back until you have something to entertain us with.'

Sandy stumbled shamefaced to the door and crept out, well aware of everyone looking at him and imagining he could hear the girls sniggering. How on earth could he face them tomorrow?

Without really thinking where he was going, he shuffled down the track that led to the river. There he found an old boat tied up. It was one that wasn't used anymore and the bottom was full of water. It didn't look too rotten though. Sandy pulled some brambles away and stepped in. Luckily he was wearing his tackety boots – heavy boots with hobnails in the soles to stop them wearing out. They were the only boots he had and they kept the water out and stopped his feet from getting wet. Just for something to do, Sandy reached under the seat and took out an old tin can that was kept there to bale water out. He started to bale and soon the water had almost gone. The boat seemed quite sound, no more water was coming in. Then he felt a jolt as it moved away from the bank. It was moving by itself with no help from him. Sandy wasn't scared but he was a bit worried because he didn't have any oars, but the river wasn't running too fast and he didn't think he would come to harm. The boat kept going, moving towards the middle of the river as though it was being steered by some invisible force. Now Sandy did begin to worry. He didn't want to go too far. He'd never been down the river and didn't know where it would take him. He'd never been across to the other side either. As he looked around wondering what to do he glanced at his legs and, instead of corduroy trousers and great big boots he saw a skirt and dainty shoes. He looked over the side of the boat at his reflection and a woman's face with red lips and long, curly hair smiled back at him! He felt around his body and, although he was not that familiar with women's bodies, he knew enough to realise that he now had one.

Then, suddenly the boat grounded on the far shore. Sandra jumped out and tried to pull it up out of the water so that it didn't drift away, but she wasn't strong enough. At that moment a young man came by and offered to lend a hand. He pulled the boat up on to the beach with no trouble at all and, seeing that the young woman seemed upset and confused, he took her back to his house, which was nearby. After a hot drink and a bowl of soup, Sandra began to feel better. It also seemed less strange to be a woman.

Because she was still muddled, had nowhere to go, and didn't even know where she was, the young man said she could stay the night. He gave her his bed while he slept downstairs in front of the fire.

When morning came, Sandra still had no idea what to do, so she just stayed. She stayed for days and weeks and months and in that time she and the young man fell in love. After a while they got married and then they had a baby and they were very happy. Sandra had completely forgotten her previous life and it was as if she had always lived there.

Then one day she went out for a walk, just to get a breath of fresh air, and her feet took her down to the riverbank where she saw an old boat. She had no memory of ever having seen the boat before but she stepped into it and felt under the seat and pulled out an old can.

20

She started to bale and the boat gave a jerk and drifted away from the shore. There were no oars and Sandra was terrified. She started to scream and yell and call for her husband, 'Oh my husband, Oh my baby. Oh my husband, Oh my baby.' He came rushing out but by now the boat was too far away and he could do nothing. Sandra slumped on to the seat and put her head in her hands … and felt a stubbly beard on her chin. When she looked down she saw corduroy trousers and great big boots. A few minutes later when the boat ran ashore, he was still shouting, 'Oh my husband, Oh my baby. Oh my husband, Oh my baby.'

Sandy was still shouting when he reached the barn where the harvest song was in full swing …

> Then drink, boys, drink!
> And see that you do not spill,
> For if you do, you shall drink two,
> For that is our Master's will …

Then the crowd began to thump on the table while the person whose turn it was downed his glass of ale and Sandy opened the door … 'Oh my husband, Oh my baby. Oh my husband, Oh my baby.' he yelled and silence fell as everyone turned to look at him.

The Master rose and went to him and put his arm round him. 'Sandy, what's happened? Where have you been? What are you shouting about?'

He gave Sandy a glass of ale to calm him and insisted on Sandy telling everyone what had happened.

So Sandy told them the story that I have just told you and the Master said, 'Well, that's the best story we've had all night. I don't know how you came up with it but it deserves the prize,' and he gave the purse to Sandy.

Sandy went and sat in a corner and didn't say another word all night but he had a lot to think about.

A transgender story usually known as 'Tackety Boots' that comes from the traveller community in Scotland. When I started to write it, it took over and insisted on expanding!

ON MINSTRELS, BARDS AND THE LIKE

Minstrels, bards, troubadours, jongleurs or just plain street singers …
and, for that matter, folk singers and storytellers of the present day,
have all played a role in both preserving the old traditions and adding
new material to them. In this book you'll find a mixture of stories,
some of which Glasgerion himself might have known and performed,
alongside some much more recent material of which I hope he would
have approved.

Glasgerion is described as a 'bard'. A bard was much more than
just a musician or storyteller. He was also a verse maker, a composer,
a story maker, a historian, a genealogist and a teacher. I don't know
whether there were ever female bards, I suspect not, but in the much
more informal environment of the family today it is usually one of
the women folk who hold the family history, literally sometimes in
the form of the photograph albums.

A minstrel or bard would need a rich patron if he was to make a
good living but sometimes the life of a street entertainer was the lesser
of two evils. If you could make however humble a living by travelling

from town to town or fair to fair entertaining people with songs, stories or animal acts it might have seemed better than staying put and starving. But then perhaps, after a while, the gloss would wear off and you would begin to miss your home and family and decide it wasn't so bad after all, as this song describes. I love the image of the children rushing out to meet him with their 'prittle-prattling stories'.

SPENCER THE ROVER

These words were composed by Spencer the Rover
Who had travelled Great Britain and most parts of Wales,
He had been so reduced which caused great confusion
And that was the reason he went on the roam.

In Yorkshire near Rotherham he had been on his rambles,
Being weary of travelling he sat down to rest,
At the foot of yonder mountain there runs a clear fountain,
With bread and cold water he himself did refresh.

It tasted more sweeter than the gold he had wasted,
More sweeter than honey and gave more content,
But the thoughts of his babies lamenting their father
Brought tears to his eyes and caused him to lament.

The night fast approaching to the woods he resorted,
With woodbine and ivy his bed for to make,
There he dreamt about sighing, lamenting and crying,
Go home to your family and rambling forsake.

On the fifth of November I've a reason to remember,
When first he arrived home to his family and wife,
They stood so surprised when first he arrived
To see such a stranger once more in their sight.

His children came around him with their prittle-prattling stories,
With their prittle-prattling stories to drive care away,
Now they are united like birds of one feather,
Like bees in one hive contented they'll stay.

So now he is a-living in his cottage contented,
With woodbine and roses growing all around the door.
He's as happy as those that's got thousands of riches;
Contented he'll stay and go rambling no more.

Trad English. A rural idyll. Well known in the south of England as far north as Derbyshire but only collected once (traditionally) in Yorkshire itself!

BLONDEL THE MINSTREL

One of the few minstrels in Britain whose name has come down to us is Blondel, minstrel to Richard the Lionheart, although his story is almost completely a fairy tale with little substance and even less truth to it! It's one of those stories that used to turn up in books and encyclopaedias for children as an exemplar of loyalty or Britishness, or something ...

King Richard I, Richard Coeur de Lion (the Lionheart), is one of England's most famous kings despite the fact that he spent hardly any of his life in England and spoke French as his first language! He was a charismatic figure and great warrior and distinguished himself in fighting in the Crusades to try to recapture Jerusalem from the Saracens. While he was off fighting, Richard left his brother John as acting king. This is the background to all the Robin Hood stories, of course.

Richard was a natural warrior, fought well and won many battles. He gained the respect of the Saracen leader, Saladin, but infighting among the Christian leaders meant that the whole campaign was a failure.

On his way home to England, Richard was taken prisoner by Duke Leopold of Austria and imprisoned in Durnstëin Castle on the shores of the Danube to await a ransom.

It was claimed officially that neither John, nor anyone else in England, knew where Richard was being held so he could not be rescued nor his ransom paid. However, his minstrel and great friend, Blondel, vowed he would find him and went round Europe, from castle to castle, palace to palace, singing the first verse of a song that he and Richard had composed together and no one else knew. After months of travelling, Blondel was rewarded when a voice answered his singing by adding the second verse. Richard had been found, the ransom was paid, and he was able to return to England.

In fact, John must have known all along where Richard was being held – how else would he have been able to pay the ransom! It wasn't paid because John was enjoying himself too much being King of England. Whether Blondel did find him, and whether he actually existed, is open to question but it makes a good story!

Even the Ladybird book of Richard I admits that most of this story is not true, even though it does pretend to be history!

ROBIN HOOD AND ALAN-A-DALE

Come listen to me, you gallants so free,
All you that loves mirth for to hear,
And I will you tell of a bold outlaw,
That lived in Nottinghamshire.

Early one summer's morning, Robin Hood was out wandering through his beloved Sherwood Forest. He had no particular purpose in mind, he was just looking round and making sure everything was as it should be. He was keeping an eye out for any strangers or any sign that the Sheriff of Nottingham or any of the other nobility or churchmen in the area were oppressing the people. He also wanted to know if any of the poor folk who lived in the forest were suffering in any way because, if they were, he could sometimes help them.

He paused and stood behind a tree as he heard the sound of someone coming along the path. It was a young man. He was almost skipping along in a jaunty fashion as though he was the happiest man in the world. He was dressed in the multicoloured garb of a minstrel, on his back was a harp and he was singing to himself – a merry love song. Robin smiled to himself, this was a young man who was head-over-heels in love, and he remained standing in the shadows until he had disappeared round the bend.

The next morning, Robin was standing in the same place at the same time and the same young man came by again but this time he was shuffling along, dragging his feet and looking at the ground as though he was the saddest man in the world. He had changed from his merry clothing into a worn and patched brown tunic and stockings and had left his harp behind somewhere. Nor was he singing this morning, but every now and again he would sigh and murmur. It was obvious that the young man's love had, somehow, gone very wrong.

Then, out stepped Little John and Much the Miller's Son. The young man instantly drew his knife. 'Stand aside,' he said. 'What do you want with me?'

'You must come with us to meet our master,' said Little John.

When they came to where Robin was waiting the young man asked again what they wanted.

'Have you any spare money for my merry men and me?'

'All I have is five shillings and a ring which I have kept for seven years to use at my wedding. Yesterday I was to be married to the sweetest young lady in the world – the Lady Christabel. She would have married me and we would have been happy – but her father did not approve. He has arranged instead for her to marry an old man! A rich old knight; one of his friends and a lackey of the Sheriff. We are both heartbroken but I can do nothing about it.'

Robin felt sorry for the man, who obviously meant every word of what he said, and he was also eager to do anything that might upset the Sheriff. 'What will you give me if I help you marry your true love?' he asked.

'I have no money and no estates, I have nothing to give you, but I promise that, if you can help me, I will forever be your loyal servant.'

Then Robin asked where the wedding was to be and was told it was only 5 miles off in the tiny hamlet of Papplewick, so he set off at top speed. When he reached the church he saw that there was a small crowd assembled, dressed ready for a wedding. Robin's old enemy, the Bishop of Hereford, was waiting at the door in all his regalia but he didn't recognise Robin and hailed him and asked who he was.

'I am a bold harper,' said Robin, 'the finest in the North Country.'

'I love the music of a harp,' said the Bishop, 'come give us a tune while we wait.'

'I will not give you a tune until I see the bride and groom.'

After a short wait there came along a group of people led by an old, bent, wrinkled, grey-haired knight and behind him a fair young lass who shone like the summer sun.

'If this is the bride and groom then it is no fit match,' cried Robin. 'You can't marry this child to this doddery old fool! The bride must choose her own husband.'

Then Robin put his horn to his mouth and blew three loud blasts. Within minutes his merry men appeared with Alan-a-Dale at their head. 'This is the man she wants to marry,' said Robin and from the way the couple embraced it was obvious to all that this was true.

'I can't do it, I won't,' stuttered the Bishop. 'The banns must be called. They have already been read three times in the church so if there is to be a wedding it must be between the two appointed people.'

With that Robin ripped off the Bishop's cloak and put it on Little John. 'By my troth,' he said. 'If manners make a man so do clothes! I have now made you a Bishop. Do your work,' and Little John climbed into the pulpit and asked seven times, in case three wasn't enough, if anyone knew why these two young people should not be married. The congregation roared with laughter and clapped their hands and the Bishop had no alternative but to marry them.

After the service they all retired to Robin's camp, where a great feast was served. True to his word, Alan-a-Dale and his wife Christabel were loyal friends to Robin and his men for many years and helped him in some of his most famous escapades. On his death, Alan was buried in the churchyard at Papplewick.

And thus having ended this merry wedding,
The bride lookt as fresh as a queen,
And so they returnd to the merry green wood,
Amongst the leaves so green.

Taken from Child#138, which was taken in turn from a seventeenth-century broadside. Alan-a-Dale was a minstrel who joined Robin's merry men. At first he was a minor character but he has grown in importance over the years. There is a plaque to him in Papplewick churchyard.

THE TWO SISTERS

A minstrel is no good without his instrument. This ballad tells how he
made himself a new one from the most unlikely of materials!

There were two sisters who lived in a bower
Hey, ho, sing nanny-O
There came a knight to be their wooer
And the swan it swims so bonny-O

He courted the one with gloves and rings …
But he loved the youngest above everything …

He courted the eldest with brooch and knife …
But he loved the youngest above his own life …

She took her sister by the hand …
And she led her down to the river's strand …

The youngest sister she stood upon a stone …
And the eldest sister she pushed her in the foam.

O sister, O sister pray give me your hand …
And I will give you houses and land …

I'll neither give you hand nor glove …
Unless you give me your own true love …

Sometimes she sank, sometimes she swam …
Until she came to the miller's dam …

And the miller's daughter all dressed in red …
She's gone for some water to make her bread …

O father, O father draw up your dam …
For there's either a mermaid or a milk-white swan …

They laid her on the bank to dry …
There came a minstrel passing by.

And he's taken out her white breast-bone …
Said 'That'll make a fiddle that'll play a fine tune.'

And he took off her fingers so fair …
Said 'These'll make pegs for my fiddle so rare.'

And he took four strands of her long yellow hair …
Said 'These'll make strings for my fiddle so fair.'

He went into her father's hall …
To play the fiddle before them all …

And the first tune it played was My Father the King …
And the second tune it played was My Mother the Queen …

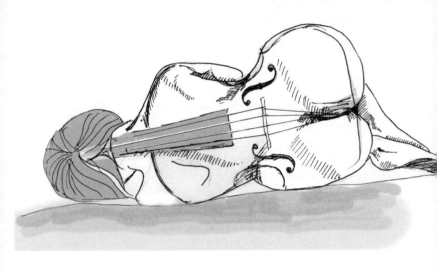

And the third tune it played was My Sister Joan …
For she it was that pushed me in the foam …

They built up a fire that would near burn stone
Hey, ho, sing nanny-O
And into the middle they pushed her sister Joan
And the swan it swims so bonny-O.

*'The Two (or Twa) Sisters' (Child#10); also known as 'The Cruel Sister',
'The Barkshire Tragedy', 'The Swan Swims So Bonny-O' and 'Binnorie'.
Child collected over eighty versions of the ballad and there are many more. I
have sung three over the years. It is widely sung in the folk revival. The story
always remains the same but the chorus lines and tunes can be very different.
Versions of the story are widespread throughout Europe. The instrument the
minstrel makes is sometimes a harp and sometimes a fiddle. I suspect that the
harp in the older versions was superseded by the fiddle in more modern times.*

*It goes to show that you can't trust a wandering minstrel, you never know
what they'll get up to!*

BINNORIE

There were two sisters, quite close in age. They were the daughters of a nobleman. The elder one was being courted by a young knight. As the weeks and months passed he came to know and become fond of her younger sister too, in a platonic way – she was his girlfriend's little sister – but the older girl grew jealous. There was probably no reason, he wasn't going to move his affections from one to the other, but love can do strange things to one. The man would bring them presents – gloves, rings, handkerchiefs and, somehow, the older one began to think that her little sister's presents were always better or meant more than the ones he gave her. She began to hate her sister and wish she wasn't there. She even thought of killing her, but how could she do it?

Then, one day, the two girls found themselves walking along the river bank. It was a large, fast-flowing river and ever since they were tiny it had been drilled into them to keep away from the edge and to be careful about not falling in because, if they did, they knew they would be swept away and probably drowned.

The older sister saw her chance. She called her sister over to look at a fish just under the bank and, when she stood on the edge to see properly, she gave her a push and she plunged in.

The young girl splashed about. She couldn't swim, and even if she had been able to she would have been weighed down by her long skirts and petticoats.

'Help,' she called. 'Sister, give me your hand.'

'I won't give you hand nor glove,' she said, 'for if I do you'll steal away my own true love.'

'Sister, sister, save my life. I do not want your own true love.'

'If I save your life your pretty face, your golden hair, your slender waist will mean I can never relax while you are around. I will never be able to trust my husband and I will always be wondering where he is, and where you are, and if you two are together.'

The young girl in the water pleaded and promised that she would have nothing to do with the young man. She would go away, she would join a nunnery … but by now it was too late. She had drifted into the current and it suddenly took hold of her and swept her away downstream. There was no way she could have been saved even if the older girl had wanted to.

The drowning girl's body floated down the river until it was washed into the leat of a mill. The miller's daughter happened to see it and, at

first, thought it was a swan but then realised it was a woman's body. She didn't know if she was alive or dead but she quickly called to her father to draw up the dam to stop the body being taken up by the mill wheel. They pulled the body out of the water and found she was dead so they laid her out on the bank.

At that moment a minstrel came wandering by and saw the body lying there. He looked at it and thought, 'I could make a fine harp from that body! A harp which would play fine music.'

He took out her breastbone and used it for the frame of the harp. Then he took her fingers and used them for pegs. The strings he made from her braided hair. When he ran his fingers over them it made a strange, beautiful, haunting music in which you could imagine words.

The minstrel took the harp into her father's hall and started to play but instead of the songs he wanted to play, the harp sang songs of its own.

The first song told about the young woman's father; the second song about her mother; and the third song was about her older sister. It told of how she had pushed her in the river in her jealousy. The father ordered a fire to be built and she was tied to a stake and burned.

Joseph Jacobs retells the above story in English Fairy Tales *(1890) as 'Binnorie', taken from the chorus line of one variant of the ballad. He has obviously used the ballad as his starting point because he uses phrases taken from it throughout as well as quoting the occasional verse. I have followed his lead.*

The manufacturing of a musical instrument from a body, or bodies, is common in stories throughout the world. Two quick examples: in India there is the story of 'Little Ankle Bone' and later in this book there is 'The Gypsy Violin' from Transylvania. I suppose you could do it ... Stone Age man made whistles from the bones of birds. A man falling in love with his girlfriend's little sister was a common motif in 1950s/60s pop songs. Chuck Berry, Elvis Presley and The Loving Spoonful all did such songs, as did many others.

THE RAGGLE TAGGLE GYPSIES-O

aka The Gypsy Laddie, Seven Yellow Gypsies and Various Other Titles

This is one of the best known of the 'Child Ballads'. Just about every folk singer in the English-speaking world seems to have sung it. There are versions from all over Britain, and in America it has become Black Jack Davy – strumming on his big guitar! I suppose the idea of a 'Lady' leaving her lord and running off with someone who comes singing at her gate appeals to musicians!

The version I've included here is a pretty standard one but they don't vary too much apart from the chorus – if they have one. The most popular version is 'The Whistling Gypsy Rover', which was a top forty hit for the Highwaymen in the early 1960s and has been recorded by The Corries, The Clancy Brothers, The Seekers and many others.

The chorus goes:

Ah de do, Ah de do da day, Ah de do ah de day
He whistled and he sang till the green woods rang
And he won the heart of a lady.

The one I sing is much less jolly and doesn't include any singing, so I didn't use it here – it's obviously just his looks and charm that bewitch her! There is a long tradition that the ballad is based on real events concerning Lord Cassillis and Johnny Faa, the King of the Gypsies, so that follows:

Three Gypsies came round to my door,
Downstairs ran my lady-o.
One sang high and one sang low
And one sang Bonny Bonny Biscay-o.

Then she took off her silken gown
And dressed in hose of leather-o.
The dirty rags around my door
She's gone with the raggle-taggle Gypsies-o.

Twas late last night when the lord came home
Enquiring for his lady-o,
The servants replied on every side
She's gone with the raggle-taggle Gypsies-o.

Go harness me my milk white steed,
Go and fetch my pony-o,
And I will ride to seek my bride
Who's gone with the raggle-taggle Gypsies-o.

And he rode high and he rode low,
He rode through woods and copses-o,
He rode 'til he came to a wide open field
And there he espied his lady-o.

What makes you leave your houses and lands
What makes you leave your money-o
What makes you leave your new wedded lord
To go with the raggle-taggle Gypsies-o?

What care I for my houses and lands,
What care I for my money-o,
What care I for my new wedded lord
When I can go with the raggle-taggle Gypsies-o?

Last night you slept in a goose-feather bed
With the sheets turned down so bravely-o,
Tonight you'll lie in the cold open field
In the arms of the raggle-taggle Gypsies-o.

What care I for my goose-feather bed
With the sheets turned down so bravely-o?
I'd rather lie in the cold open field
In the arms of the raggle-taggle Gypsies-o.

The Raggle Taggle Gypsies-O Child#200

JOHNNY FAA

The True Story of the Raggle Taggle Gypsies-O

John, the 6th Earl of Cassillis, took as his wife Lady Jean Hamilton, the daughter of the 1st Earl of Haddington. Lady Jean had previously been courted by Sir John Faa of Dunbar and she loved him but his position in society was not acceptable to her father. The marriage between Lady Jean and Cassillis was very much a marriage made for family connections and position in society rather than love or affection – the position of the wider family, not just Jean.

Cassillis took Lady Jean to live at Cassillis Castle, a huge old tower on the banks of the River Doon near Maybole in Ayrshire.

In the next few years Lady Jane gave Cassillis three children but was dreadfully unhappy and could not forget her previous lover. He obviously did not forget her either.

When Cassillis went on matters of government to an Assembly of Divines in faraway Westminster, Sir John enlisted three gypsies to help him, disguised himself as a gypsy, and went to Cassillis Castle, where he made himself known to Jean. (Whether he did this by serenading her outside her window, as in the song, or not I will leave to your imagination!) It did not take much persuading for her to agree to run away with him.

They had not gone far before Lord Cassillis returned home unexpectedly, found out what had happened and set off in pursuit. He took with him a large band of troops and they had no trouble in catching the runaways at a ford over the Doon just a few miles from the castle – a place now called the Gypsies' Steps. They overpowered Johnny Faa and his men and took them back to the castle. Sir John and the three gypsies were hanged on the 'Dule Tree', a huge plane tree that still stands in front of the castle. Lady Jean was forced to watch the hanging from a window in her room. Later she was taken away and imprisoned in a house at Maybole and the Earl of Cassillis, while she was still alive, married someone else.

'Such is the legend of the love-lorn lady and her gallant Gypsy which all Minniebolers swear to be true, but "facts are chiels that winna ding" and the truth is there is no truth in the story.' (Robert Chambers, *A Picture of Scotland*, 1828.) In fact, Sir John Cassillis and Lady Jean lived happily together for twenty years.

Johnny Faa was a historical character but he lived a hundred years before Sir John and Lady Jean Cassillis. King James V gave him authority over all the Gypsies of Scotland and made him the unofficial 'Lord and Earl of Little Egypt' (as he is in Philip Pullman's His Dark Materials*).*

For some reason Johnny Faa, Lady Jean and Lord Cassillis became identified with what was already an old ballad. It's the kind of thing that happens regularly and once the story is fixed it is impossible to persuade people that it isn't true!

SINGING SAM OF DERBYSHIRE

It is open to argument whether the tales of Robin Hood, the Two Sisters and the other 'big ballads' included here were written by professional musicians and then filtered down to the lower classes, or if it was the other way round – were they made up by common people and later 'improved' for the gentry? Whichever it was, they were distributed around the villages, not by minstrels but by a much more humble kind of travelling entertainer like Singing Sam, described by Llewellynn Jewitt in his 1867 book *The Ballads and Songs of Derbyshire* (which is, of course, part of Robin Hood's territory).

As a frontispiece to my present volume, I give a facsimile of an old portrait of a Derbyshire ballad-singer of the last century, 'Singing Sam of Derbyshire', as he was called, which I copy from the curious plate etched by W. Williams in 1760, which appeared in 'The Topographer' thirty years after that time. The man was a singular character – a wandering minstrel who got his living by singing ballads in the Peak villages, and accompanying himself on his rude single-stringed instrument. Doubtless The Beggar's Ramble and The Beggar's Wells and other similar rhymes were the production of Singing Sam or his compeers, and recounted his own peregrinations through the country. His instrument was as quaint and curious as himself. It consisted of a straight staff nearly as tall as himself, with a single string tied fast around it at each end. This he tightened with a fully inflated cow's bladder, which assisted very materially the tone of the rude instrument. His bow was a rough stick of hazel or briar, with a single string and with this, with the lower end of his staff resting on the ground, and the upper grasped by his right hand, which he passed up and down to tighten or slacken the string as he played, he scraped away, and produced sounds which, though not so musical as those of Paganini and his single string, would no doubt harmonize with Sam's rude ballad, and ruder voice.

(Sam's instrument is not unlike the tea chest bass used in 1950s skiffle groups.)

Here is an extract from 'The Beggar's Ramble' mentioned above. I won't include too much as it is more of a gazetteer than a story! But many of us who perform songs or stories have found that if you mention a particular place you are certain to get a cheer from members of the audience who happen to come from there, so if you mention a list of places you have pleased a lot of people – and that's what you are trying to do!

The Beggars Ramble (Extract)

Hark ye well, my neighbours all, and pray now can you tell
Which is the way unto the Beggar's Well?
There is Eaton, and Toton, and Brancot on the hill,
There's Beggerly Beaston, and lousy Chilwell,

There's Trowel, and there's Cosel, from there to Cimberly Knowl,
I would have call'd at Watnall, but I thought it would not do,
There's Beaver, and there's Hansley, & so for Perkin Wood,
I meant to have call'd at Selson, but there ale is not good,

There's Snelson green, and Pinstone green, and Blackwell old hall,
An old place where I had lived I had a mind to call;
I got a good refreshment, and something else beside,
So turning up the closes, South Normanton I 'spied …

The list continues through verse after verse but he never appears to arrive at his destination!

'Singing Sam of Derbyshire' is from The Ballads and Songs of Derbyshire *by Llewellynn Jewitt, 1867.*

Another Derbyshire collector and antiquarian, Sidney Oldall Addy, stated:

It is very likely that folk-tales were distributed in England by wandering pedlars, tinkers and merchants, many of whom came from foreign lands … I might refer to the old Norse *umrenningr*, the land-louper, who went from house to house distributing news and tales, and in short performing the office of a walking newspaper and story book.

THE OLD WANDERING DROLL-TELLER OF THE LIZARD, AND HIS STORY OF THE MERMAID AND THE MAN OF CURY (PRONOUNCED CURIE)

Songs and stories were spread around in Derbyshire by Singing Sam and there were probably people like him playing a similar role in most parts of the country: entertaining at local events, carrying songs, stories and news, keeping traditions alive and, where nothing relevant already existed, making a new song or story for the occasion.

In West Cornwall the man who had taken on that position was called Anthony James. Uncle Anthony, as he was known, had been a soldier when he was younger but was now old and blind so, with his dog and a boy who acted as his guide, he toured the countryside every year following a set route from which he never varied. He would visit the same places at the same time every year and probably tell the same stories that everyone knew by heart, but they didn't mind; they liked to hear them again and again and there was, occasionally, a new droll – which is what they called the stories – or perhaps a song or ballad he had found or made to add a bit of variety to the programme. He accompanied himself on a crwth, an ancient fiddle, and specialised in stories about the people of the area, particularly the white witches of Cury. They were the Lutey family and this, Uncle Anthony's favourite story, tells how they came by their powers.

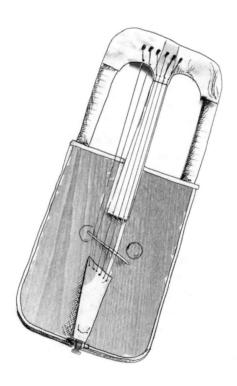

THE MERMAID AND
THE MAN OF CURY

Hundreds of years ago a man named Lutey, who lived near Lizard Point, finished his day's work and wandered down to the beach to see if anything worthwhile had been washed up by the sea. Like most of the people in the area, Lutey farmed a little bit of land, did some fishing and, occasionally, indulged in a bit of smuggling. It was always worth doing a bit of beachcombing as well because you never knew what you might find. Often it was just a useful bit of rubbish, but now and again ...

This day he didn't find anything and had turned to go home when he heard the sound of singing – well, was it singing? or was it wailing? or was it a child crying? He wasn't quite sure, but he made his way towards it. He went round some rocks near the sea, which would have been under water at high tide, and there was the most beautiful woman he had ever seen. All he could see of her was her head and shoulders and her upper back because she was half-immersed in a rock pool, but he could tell that she was naked. He watched her for a while and then coughed so that he didn't come upon her unawares. At this she instantly slid into the pool so that just her head was sticking out.

'Don't be scared,' said Lutey, 'I won't harm you. I'm a happily married man. (This was almost true, he was married but I don't know how happily, and as for not harming her … well it depended on what you mean and what was going to happen next.) Have you lost your clothes – I don't see them anywhere?'

The woman didn't reply and Lutey went closer and looked into the pool where he saw a long, fish-like tail. He realised she was a mermaid. He had never seen one close up before although he had caught glimpses and had heard them singing out at sea.

'Don't be scared,' he said again, 'Can you understand me? I don't know whether you know our good Cornish language …'

'I understand you very well. We people of the ocean know many languages because we live all round your shores and all your peoples cross our oceans. We can also hear you talking on land from many miles out when we are at home, so we know all about you. It's you who might be scared,' she continued, 'to see me here clad in nothing but my natural skin when all your women wear those big, heavy, ugly garments which make it impossible to swim and sport in the sea.'

'Oh, I'm not scared to see a naked woman,' bragged Lutey. 'Just come out of the pool so that I can see you properly to continue our conversation.'

The mermaid did as he asked, she slid up out of the water and on to a rock, but her hair hung round her like a curtain so she might just as well have been fully clothed in those big, heavy, ugly garments. Lutey was disappointed!

The mermaid sighed and told Lutey that she was frightened because she had been careless and got herself stranded in a pool far from the sea – a thing a mermaid had drummed into her from when she was very young that you should never allow to happen. She had left her husband sleeping at home and she should go to him.

'Well, stay and talk to me,' said Lutey, 'I will stay here and look after you until the tide comes in.'

'I have often wished I could have a conversation with your people,' said the mermaid, 'but I cannot wait until the tide returns.'

She was frightened that if she didn't get home soon, she said, her husband might wake up and feel hungry and then he might eat her children because mermaid children are very small and mermen do that sort of thing.

'My husband will wake up, and if I am not there with a fine catch of fish, then he will start to whistle and all my children will come to him because they love music, and he will lure them closer and closer until they are all around his lips and then he will suck them in and chew them up. If mermen did not behave in that way then we would be as numerous as herrings! It will soon be low tide and I must be home by then, but I cannot get back to the sea.'

Lutey said he would like to help.

'Just carry me back to the sea,' she said, 'and I will reward you handsomely. Take this …' and she reached for a comb that was hidden in her hair. 'If ever you need my help just pass it three times through the sea and call my name and I will be there on the next high tide.'

So Lutey picked up the mermaid in his arms and carried her towards the sea. He was very aware that he held a naked woman in his arms but he tried to banish the thought. He was a powerful man and she weighed very little so it was easy for him. As they walked she told him that her name was Morwenna, which means woman of the sea, and Lutey was charmed by her lithe body, her flute-like voice and her sea-green eyes, and he would have done anything for her.

At length they reached the edge of the sea where the small ripples were dancing over the sand and Lutey stopped, preparing to put her down.

'What three things would you like me to grant you now?' she asked, 'three wishes …' It took Lutey a minute to realise what she meant and he thought carefully. Images flashed through his mind from stories he'd heard where men had wasted their wishes and finished up with nothing or with something worthless … Lutey was basically a good man and he thought about his friends and neighbours and how hard their lives sometimes were and how, if he was clever, he could make his three wishes help them as well as himself, so he thought carefully …

His first wish was that he would be able to break the spells of witchcraft; second, that he may have such power over familiar spirits as to compel them to inform him of all he needed to know for the benefit of others, and third, that these good gifts may be passed down in his family forever.

The mermaid was very pleased that Lutey had made such wise and unselfish choices and promised that his wishes would come true and, in addition, none of his family would ever come to harm in the sea.

Then she begged Lutey to come with her to her home under the sea and she listed all the wonders that he would find there, the beautiful corals and fishes, the wrecks full of treasure and strange things that were washed down from the land – and all the beautiful mermaids who would make Lutey very welcome indeed. And she would be there with him of course … She painted such a beautiful picture that Lutey was very tempted until he thought about being in an under-sea world. He said that he would drown within a few minutes of going under the water but she assured him that she could give him gills so that he could live there perfectly comfortably and she continued to speak in her sing-song voice, which became more and more like music weaving a spell around him.

By now Lutey was up to his knees in the sea and had almost made up his mind to keep walking and to carry her on into her world and stay with her for the rest of his days. A few more steps and he was waist deep.

But, just then Lutey's dog, who had been following them, barked from the shore and Lutey turned and he saw the hills of his native land, and his cottage with smoke rising from the chimney, and a line of washing swaying in the breeze. He thought of his wife and children and his friends and his everyday life. Did he want to swap all that for a life under the sea where mermen eat their own children? He realised that he was being enchanted and taken where he did not want to go. He suddenly hated her cold, eel-like body and her hair like seaweed. Her voice sounded like the screech of gulls and her breath was like rotten fish. He drew his knife: 'Let me go,' he shouted, 'or I will gut you like a herring!' Whether it was the threat, or the fact that cold steel will often ward off magic, she dropped from his arms and plunged into the sea. As she swam off she turned and called, 'Farewell, my love; for nine long years; after which I'll return for you.'

Lutey barely had the strength to make his way back to the dry sand and into a small cave where he always kept a few barrels of rum hidden under other bits of the wreckage he found. After a quick drink he fell into a deep sleep.

His wife had a restless night wondering where he could be. He sometimes stayed out all night if there was some mischief afoot but he usually let her know and he hadn't been back for either supper or breakfast. So, as soon as the sun was up, she went down to the shore and into the cave, where she found Lutey fast asleep. She assumed he was drunk and sleeping it off, so she roughly roused him.

He didn't know where he was. 'Are you Morwenna? Have you taken me to your home after all?' he asked.

'I don't know this Morwenna you're talking about,' she replied. 'I'm your wife and they call me Aunt Betty Lutey and if you don't get yourself home pretty quick you'll feel my boot behind you!'

As they went home, Lutey begged for forgiveness and told his wife all that had happened and how it was only the barking of their good old dog that had prevented him from leaving her a widow. He made her promise not to tell any of the neighbours because they wouldn't understand.

Now the thing you most want to tell your friends is that thing you have promised not to tell, so as soon as Lutey went off to his work the next day Mrs Lutey went all round the neighbourhood telling everyone what had happened and making them swear in turn not to breath a word of it to anyone else. But, of course, they did and pretty soon the story had spread all over Cornwall. Soon after that people started to come to consult Lutey to see whether the gifts the mermaid had promised were real and, to his surprise, Lutey discovered they were. He was able to help them in many ways and far better than any normal white witch could. This continued for years and then, nine years to the day from when he had carried the mermaid down to the sea, Lutey and a friend were out fishing. It was a dead calm, peaceful, moonlit night and the fishing was going well when suddenly the water near the boat heaved and the mermaid rose up from out of the water with her long hair trailing behind her. She reached out her hand and Lutey took it, slid into the sea, and disappeared with her. His body was never found.

From that time on, the Lutey family have been known as healers and wise men. In fact the whole area around Cury is famous for its healers.

The only downside to the arrangement seems to be that once every nine years a member of the Lutey family is mysteriously lost at sea, so perhaps the mermaid did not entirely keep her word.

Based on: Traditions and Hearthside Stories of West Cornwall, Vol. 1, *by William Bottrell, 1870, at sacred-texts.com. Mike O'Connor also based his History Press book* Cornish Folk Tales *(2010) on the wanderings and tales of Uncle Anthony. I read it when it first came out but deliberately did not refer to it again now!*

As the title says, Cury is pronounced 'Curie' and the instrument, the crwth, is pronounced 'crowd'.

THE MERMAID
OF ZENNOR

Another mermaid legend from Cornwall but this one is much better known. Local legends, when they take root, are jealously guarded and woe betide anyone who dares to question them or say that it might not have been quite like that. There is often a lot riding on it and if the legend ceased to be told then the whole community would suffer.

Long ago, in the little village of Zennor, which is just inland from the north coast of Cornwall not far from St Ives, a finely dressed woman would occasionally attend services at St Senara's Church. Her visits were intermittent and sometimes weeks or months would pass between them and no one knew who she was or where she came from. Locals like a good gossip, of course, and some are naturally nosy and want to know all about everyone, so some of them tried to follow her when she left the church, or they watched her from the summit of the nearby Trearthen Hill, but she always seemed to disappear without them seeing exactly where she went. She obviously didn't live locally but they wondered whether she was a relative of someone who did or whether she just liked visiting the area, or what …? Her visits continued for some years but she didn't show any sign of ageing. She still seemed a young and beautiful woman although she wore long dresses and a veil so people only caught occasional glimpses of her face. What was beyond argument was that she had a beautiful voice.

Another fine singer who attended the church regularly was Matthew Trewella, the son of the church warden. He had a rich bass voice and it became the custom that he would sing a hymn to close the service.

One day the strange woman was so overcome by the beauty of his singing that she allowed her veil to slip and gazed at him with love-filled eyes. He was instantly smitten and followed her from the church. Neither of them was ever seen again.

Several years later a ship anchored in Pendour Cove, very near to Zennor, and a short while later a mermaid appeared beside it and asked if the anchor could be raised because it was blocking the door to her home and she couldn't get in to feed her children. The sailors knew it is best never to upset mermaids so they instantly raised the anchor and sailed away.

When the people of Zennor heard this their imaginations worked overtime and they assumed that it was the same woman who had visited their church and who had enticed Matthew Trewella away. She must have lured him to her home beneath the waves, they said, and they were living there and raising a family.

Some say that, to this day, they can be heard singing together under the waves and that their singing tells the local fishermen whether the sea is going to be calm or rough.

From various sources: a very well-known Cornish folk tale that was first recorded by the folklorist William Bottrell in 1873. Some say he wrote it inspired by the strange carving of a mermaid on the end of a pew in St Senara's Church. It is hard to say which is the older – the pew or the story. The legend has inspired works of poetry, literature, music and art, and is the basis of the whole local tourist industry.

ION THE FIDDLER

Ion the Fiddler had been playing at a 'merry night' in a neighbouring village. It had gone on late and it was well past midnight when he was eventually able to put his fiddle in its case and head for home. At first he was wide awake and full of adrenalin because of the excitement of the evening but gradually it began to wear off and he felt more and more tired. He even felt himself nodding off as he walked. He thought he was going along by the usual route, the one he'd followed many times before … he went over the hill as usual and saw the lake at the bottom as usual, but beside the lake there was a large house, almost a mansion. He was sure he hadn't seen it before but it couldn't suddenly have appeared so perhaps it had been hidden by trees, or had they clipped a hedge, or demolished a wall …?

All the windows in the house were full of light even though it was so late and, as Ion came near, a finely dressed servant ran out to greet him. He invited him in. 'Come and have some refreshment,' he said.

Ion went into a huge ballroom, where he was given a glass of wine finer than any he had ever drunk before and immediately he felt fresh and full of life. He somehow knew that he was the finest fiddle player in the land! People gathered round and called him by his name, although he was sure he didn't know any of them, and they asked him to play and he played better than he'd ever played before and the people danced better than any crowd he'd ever played for before. When the dancers are good it inspires the musician to play well and that helps the dancers … and so on. After a dance or two the servant took Ion's hat and as he took it round the room the crowd filled it with gold and silver coins. Then they danced some more. This went on until nearly dawn, when they gradually drifted away. When the last couple had left Ion laid himself down on a couch and fell asleep.

When he woke up it was about midday and Ion found himself lying on a hillside in the open air. His fiddle was in its case beside him and his hat was lying where it had fallen, but instead of gold and silver coins it was full of autumn leaves. Of the mansion there was no sign and he never saw it again.

But Ion did have another adventure with the fairies, for that is what they must have been, he decided.

A year or two later he had, again, been play-ing at a lively event in a neighbouring village and was making his way home in the early hours. He had learned from his previous experience, so he was always care-ful about his route and when he realised that it was going to take him along Fairy Green Lane, Ion was a bit apprehen-sive. Just in case anything happened, he took his fiddle from its case and tuned it. Then, to keep

his spirits up, he started to play some of his favourite airs as he walked. Suddenly he felt his fiddle grow heavy and he saw that he had just passed the green where people said the fairies danced. Ion realised that the fairies had appreciated his playing and dropped a donation into his fiddle.

When he reached home his wife was still up and waiting for him. She was very angry and laid into Ion, saying that she didn't think there was any reason why he should be that late home and accusing him of drinking away all the money he had earned by his playing. This wasn't entirely unfair because Ion did like a drink and a few times he had spent money in the pub that should have gone elsewhere. Ion's wife told him that their landlord had been round and told her that if the rent wasn't paid by Friday then they'd be out. Homeless.

'I'll bet you haven't got a ha'penny in your pocket. You're hopeless. I don't know why I put up with you.'

Ion told her not to worry, 'Just go and get my fiddle and give it a shake.' She did and was amazed at the clinking of money. When she tipped it out there were gold and silver coins enough to pay the rent several times over. She didn't dare ask how Ion had come by it.

The next day, Ion took some of the money and went and paid the landlord the outstanding rent. He was amazed because Ion usually came begging for leniency and promising to pay as soon as he could. He gratefully took the money and gave Ion a receipt. Afterwards Ion went into the pub to celebrate but a short while later the landlord came storming in.

'Where did you get that money you paid me with?

'Why?' asked Ion, 'What's wrong?'

'It's all turned into cockleshells.'

'It was alright when I gave it to you,' said Ion, 'It must have been because here's the receipt, signed by you. Someone must have swapped it.'

And no one could prove otherwise, so Ion carried on drinking.

An amalgamation of two separate Welsh folk tales.

THE GUITAR PLAYER

Not many years ago, definitely within my lifetime and perhaps within yours too, way down in Mississippi in the deep south of the USA there was a young man who was a really hot blues guitar player. He was the best player of his generation for miles around and he loved to take every opportunity to go out and play. He would find somewhere to play almost every night – a party, a dance, a bar … anywhere. He was well known locally and had quite a following, particularly of young women – young men tended to be jealous!

One night he had been playing until late and he was making his way home in the moonlight. He couldn't afford a car so he was walking down the road with his guitar case in his hand. You can imagine the scene from films and commercials you've seen set in that environment – a long straight road, a field of corn on one side and a field of cotton on the other; the occasional broken-down fence post or stunted tree; nothing much else; definitely no houses …

As he was walking along thinking about how and what he'd played that evening, he became aware of footsteps behind him. He didn't fancy meeting anyone on that lonely road at that time of night, so he started to walk faster, but the footsteps behind him went faster too. He lengthened his stride and walked as fast as he could without appearing scared, but the footsteps behind gradually got closer and closer until a figure drew alongside him. It was a little old man also carrying a guitar case.

Now, when two guitarists meet – or two fiddle players, or two trombonists – any musicians in fact – they like to compare notes, admire each others' instruments and test each other's skill in an impromptu session, so they both opened their cases, took out their guitars and started to play.

They started with the basic little intro that most blues start with and they could obviously both do that so they moved on to something a bit more difficult – the classic opening riff to Chuck Berry's 'Johnny B Goode', Howling Wolf's 'Smokestack Lightning', some Muddy Waters and John Lee Hooker, even a bit of early rock 'n' roll by Bo Diddley ... That was all easy stuff, so they moved on to the less well-known songs – the train impressions of Bukka White, songs by Big Boy Crudup, who influenced the young Elvis Presley, and even something by the almost unknown Peg Leg Howell.

Whatever was chosen, they could both play it very well indeed but gradually the young man began to feel disheartened. He could play every-thing very well but he had the feeling that the old man could play it just a little bit better. He wasn't playing faster or putting in flashier bits ... if anything his playing was more simple, but there was just that 'something' about it ... it had a bit more feeling, more soul ... it contained more of the blues.

In the end the young man stopped and said, 'How come you're so good?'

The old feller replied, 'I was even better when I was alive,' and promptly disappeared.

61

It was only then that the young man realised where he was – he was at the crossroads, and not just any crossroads but that particular crossroads where Robert Johnson is reputed to have sold his soul to the devil in return for being the best blues guitarist ever.

So he threw his guitar in the ditch, went home, and became an accountant instead!

The basic outline of this story came to me back around 1980 from West Indian storyteller Madge Spencer, although she might not recognise it now as her version had no blues and no guitar playing, just a meeting on a lonely road – and a lot of terrified screaming!

THE DEVIL'S TRILL

The blues breaks many of the rules of 'proper' music (whatever that is!). Like jazz it uses 'strange' chords – dominant 7ths and things like that. If you know about music theory you may have come across the tritone, also known as 'the Devil's interval'. It's just a chord but it sounds assonant to ears brought up on classical harmony and was banned from church music. But it occurs in the blues. Perhaps that is why it is sometimes described as 'the Devil's music'.

Robert Johnson is not the only musician reputed to have made a pact with the devil, though. Another, very different one, was the great nineteenth-century Italian violinist, Paganini. Legend has it that his mother sold his soul to the devil when he was still a tiny baby so that he would grow up to be a great violinist. It obviously worked! A 2013 film, *The Devil's Violinist*, tells the story.

And then there is 'Sonata per Violino in sol minore' – 'Il Trillo del Diavolo', better known as 'The Devil's Trill'. It was written by the Italian composer Giuseppe Tartini (1692–1770) – or was it? Perhaps it was composed by Old Nick himself! This fifteen-minute piece is still considered one of the hardest pieces to play for a violinist and it contains tritone after tritone.

Tartini described how the composition came about. This is the story in his own words:

One night, in the year 1713 I dreamed I had made a pact with the devil for my soul. Everything went as I wished: my new servant anticipated my every desire. Among other things, I gave him my violin to see if he could play. How great was my astonishment on hearing a sonata so wonderful and so beautiful, played with such great art and intelligence, as I had never even conceived in my boldest flights of fantasy.

I felt enraptured, transported, enchanted: my breath failed me, and I awoke. I immediately grasped my violin in order to retain, in part at least, the impression of my dream. In vain! The music which I at this time composed is indeed the best that I ever wrote, and I still call it the Devil's Trill but the difference between it and that which so moved me is so great that I would have destroyed my instrument and have said farewell to music forever if it had been possible for me to live without the enjoyment it affords me.

If you want to try a tritone for yourself get out your instruments and try this: in the key of C it will be a sequence or chord of C/F/B or in G try G/C/F#.

THE FOX AND
THE BAGPIPES

One day a hungry fox found a set of bagpipes that someone had dropped by the road. Now, today, the bags of bagpipes are probably made of all kinds of artificial hi-tech materials, but in those times they were made of hide. The fox started to chew on the bag for he was hungry, but there was still a tiny remnant of breath in it, so when the fox bit it the drone gave a groan. The fox, surprised but not frightened, said, 'Why, here I've found both meat and music!'

Irish. Reprinted from my book Where Dragons Soar and other Animal Folk Tales of the British Isles.

That story is about a set of Irish pipes but when we think of bagpipes the image of the Scottish soldier in his kilt playing the war pipes usually springs to mind, although there are hundreds of other bagpipes in different cultures all round the world. Pipers have always played an important part in Scottish life – playing for the nobility in their castles, piping in the haggis on Burns Night and, of course, leading armies into hails of machine-gun fire armed with nothing more than their music.

COLKITTO AND THE PHANTOM PIPER

Mid-1600s … Cavaliers and Roundheads … the English Civil War … In fact it wasn't just an English war, it affected the other nations of the British Isles, too. Charles lost his head, Cromwell took charge and ordered his bloody subjugation of Ireland. In our black and white, romantic way of seeing history we tend to see it as a class war – the Royalist nobles against the plebeian Parliamentarians – but there was also the religious element of the official Anglican Church against nonconformists. So, like all civil wars, it dragged up all kinds of old enmities and excuses for going to battle and getting revenge on your neighbours for something they might or might not have done hundreds of years before. In Scotland, the religious aspect played a major part – Catholics against Covenanters, and this was an excuse to resurrect the ancient feuds between the Campbells and MacDonalds with all the other smaller, affiliated clans lined up on either side like pieces on a chess board.

The King's Scottish army, which included the MacDonalds among other clans, was led by James Graham the Earl of Montrose, while the Covenanters, or Parliamentarians, were under the command of Archibald Campbell, the Marquess of Argyll. However, the figure who has gone down in folklore is the Royalist Coll Ciotach Mac Domhnaill (Col MacDonald, the left handed) – or, as he became known in English, Colkitto.

Colkitto was a fearsome fighter and a mercenary. He stood 6ft 6in tall and was muscular and strong. He was almost an army by himself!

In return for helping the Clan MacIntyre, their chief gave Colkitto his favourite piper to support him in his campaign. One of the first things they did was to capture Duntrune Castle in Argyll from the Campbells. When it had been secured, Colkitto left just a small garrison, including the piper, and went off to fight the next battle. While he was gone the Campbells retook the castle and killed all Colkitto's men except the piper, who was made to entertain his captors.

The Campbells knew that Colkitto would eventually return to Duntrune and when, at last, his ship was seen approaching, the piper begged permission to play to greet them. He went on to the battlements and played a tune called 'Piobaireachd-dhum-Naomhaid' but deliberately made several mistakes. Colkitto, hearing the tune wafting

over the waves, was pleased at first but then he noticed the mistakes. He knew his piper would not make such simple errors, realised it was a warning, saluted him and sailed on without stopping.

The Campbells were furious and the commander of the garrison, Lady Dunstaffnage, who was known as 'the black bitch', gave orders that the piper's hands should be cut off so that he would never be able to betray anyone again. It was done with one blow of an axe and the piper died from loss of blood. The tune he played is now known as 'The Piper's Warning to His Master'.

After that, and when peace had returned to the country, people reported hearing the tune being played from the battlements when there was no piper there and the story of a ghost took root.

Many years later, in 1888, when repairs were being made to Duntrune Castle, workmen discovered a skeleton in a shallow grave and when they took it out they discovered that it was missing its hands. Whether it was the skeleton of Colkitto's loyal piper we'll never know, but they do claim that the ghost still plays and can be heard, and occasionally seen, on the battlements.

There are other ghostly pipers in Scotland too …

THE PHANTOM PIPER OF KINCARDINE

Back in 1856, Donald Sinclair and his family sailed in a small boat from their home on the Isle of Skye, aiming for the mainland. It was October and dark and wintry, one of those days when it never really gets light. As they sailed, the wind came up and the sea grew rough and Donald lost all track of the direction he was sailing in. He had no idea where land was. To comfort himself and his family, he took out his pipes and began to play a lament. After a short while he heard the same melody being played by another piper somewhere ahead, and steered the boat towards it. They safely entered the harbour at Kincardine. We don't know who the second piper was but he saved the lives of Sinclair and his family.

In 1996 the Kincardine Pipe Band started to commemorate the event. At sunset throughout July and August (except for Saturdays), a lone piper plays from the top of the lighthouse in a tradition they call 'The Phantom Piper'. On Saturdays, the band parades through the town. The custom is now over twenty years old and set to continue.

UNDERGROUND MUSIC

People are fascinated by holes in the ground, whether they be natural or man-made. If there is a cave or a tunnel we feel an irrepressible urge to explore it, even if we are, at the same time, frightened of what we might find or what might happen.

There are all kinds of tunnels in all kinds of places: some are just service entrances, some are genuinely secret passages, some are ancient, some are more modern. Most old houses had tunnels to enable either the gentry to go about their business unseen, or the servants to do their work without upsetting the delicate feelings of their betters. Most of these tunnels are quite short but there are legends about others that are thought to be miles long. They are usually surrounded by mystery and often haunted! For many years there were stories about a tunnel connecting Richmond Castle and Easby Abbey, in Yorkshire. Nobody knew for sure if it was real and, if it was, quite where it ran. At the end of the seventeenth century, some soldiers found one end of the tunnel in the castle grounds but parts of the roof near the entrance had fallen in so there was only room for a very small person to squeeze through. In true military fashion, a little drummer boy was volunteered for the task. He could just about get through. His drum was passed to him and he was ordered to walk along the tunnel beating the drum as he went so that his comrades on the surface could hear him and map the course of the tunnel. He set off and they followed his beats and rolls, the paradiddles and pataflaflas from the castle, across the Market Place to Frenchgate and then along the banks of the River Swale heading towards Easby Abbey. He seemed to be making good time and his drum beats settled down to a steady 'pa rum pum pum-pum, pa rum pum pum-pum, pa rum pum pum-pum', so the tunnel was obviously in good order once you were past the entrance, but when they reached Easby Wood, about half a mile from the abbey, the drumming suddenly stopped … and didn't start again. No one has ever found out what happened to the little drummer boy down there in the tunnel. Did he disappear down a hole in the floor? Did the roof suddenly cave in? Was there a patch of poisonous gas? I suppose archaeologists could excavate the spot and find the answer, but they never have. The place is now marked by the Little Drummer Boy Stone.

One theory regarding his disappearance, which seems a very long shot, the kind of thing a storyteller would come up with(!) concerns King Arthur, who is supposed to be sleeping under a hill somewhere in Britain, with his knights, waiting for the time when he is needed to save the country from catastrophe. Many places claim to be that spot; places in Wales, and Somerset, the Eldon Hills, and Sewingshields among others, but until he suddenly appears we have no way of knowing which it is. Perhaps the little drummer boy stumbled into the cave where Arthur was sleeping. One of the knights might have been woken by the drum and asked whether they were needed. 'Is Britain in great danger?' he would have asked. The boy would have replied no, and the knight would have told him not to wake anyone else. Perhaps he asked the boy if he'd like to join them and he accepted. So the little drummer boy might be waiting until he, and the rest of Arthur's retinue, are summoned forth to save us all from catastrophe.

North Norfolk is a popular destination for summer holidays nowadays, but in the past it was remote and empty and better known for large estates and religious foundations. In the eleventh century, a local noblewoman had a vision in which the Virgin Mary instructed her to build, in Walsingham, a replica of the house of the holy family in Nazareth. She did so and throughout the Middle Ages it was one of the most important destinations for pilgrimage in Northern Europe. In more recent times the Anglican Church has also built a shrine and organised pilgrimages to the small town.

About 3 miles from the town is Binham Priory. It was one of the oldest priories in the country and was founded by Benedictine monks. In the priory grounds was the entrance to a tunnel that people thought might lead to Walsingham but no one ever dared explore it to find out because the entrance was haunted by a ghostly black-clad monk (Benedictines wear black).

Then, by chance, one day a wandering fiddle player and his dog appeared on the scene. (Why do these musicians appear at just the right time? The pied piper when there was a plague of rats, the minstrel just in time to cannibalise the girl's body into a musical instrument in 'Binnorie' …) He heard about the tunnel and the ghost but wasn't scared off. He offered to explore it and find where it went. (I suspect he asked for a substantial payment for doing so but what it was is not recorded!)

A crowd assembled to see him off and he entered the tunnel with his dog at his heels playing jigs and reels as he went along. The crowd were able to follow his progress on the surface by the sound of the fiddle echoing up from under the ground.

They went for quite a way until they climbed a small hill and came to a point where two roads crossed and there the music suddenly stopped.

The crowd waited, assuming he was just having a rest, but when the music didn't restart they drifted back to the mouth of the tunnel at Binham. Several hours later, the fiddler's dog rushed from the mouth of the tunnel with its tail between its legs and all its hair standing on end. It kept running and where it eventually stopped I don't know. The fiddler was never seen again.

Soon after that there was a tremendous storm and the mouth of the tunnel collapsed, so no one else has been able to follow the fiddler. Over the years the little hill where the music stopped became known as Fiddler's Hill.

Strangely, in 1933, the road around Fiddler's Hill was widened and they excavated three skeletons, one of which was a dog!

Two very similar local legends from Yorkshire and Norfolk. There are similar stories elsewhere. Both stories were put together from various sources.

FFARWEL NED PUGH

or The Disappearance of Iolo ap Hugh

In North Wales, not far from Wrexham, there is a cave that people, in the past, believed was an entrance into an enchanted underworld. If you ventured in you could travel underground all the way from Owain Glyndwr's fortress at Sycharth to Chirk Castle. But this was not something undertaken lightly; the cave had an evil reputation. No one would venture near it unless they had to. It was believed to have a sort of magnetic power, so that if you passed a particular point you would be drawn in, never to return. Even animals sensed this. One day, a fox was being pursued by the hunt and it was chased towards the cave but, rather than enter, it turned and leapt into the midst of the hounds.

Tantalised by the stories about the cave, and perhaps tempted by the money he could make from telling of his adventures, a travelling crwth player named Iolo ap Hugh in Welsh, or Ned Pugh if you were an English speaker, from Wrexham, decided to explore the cave. He announced well in advance that he would begin his adventure at midday on Halloween. He made sure there was an appreciative crowd to watch him and probably passed the hat round beforehand! He had armed himself with 7lb of candles and a plentiful supply of bread and cheese because he didn't know how long it would take him and, at 12 noon, he ventured into the cave mouth. There he turned and waved. (How he carried all the food and candles and waved and still managed to play his crwth I don't know!)

The crowd hung around waiting for something to happen. It would take him many hours to reach Chirk and return – or perhaps he would find an exit at Chirk and reappear there. More likely they expected a terrified Ned Pugh to come running out of the cave after a few minutes, or half an hour, or perhaps an hour ... But nothing happened. Ned Pugh was never seen or heard of again.

Or was he?

Elias ap Evan was a notorious drunk. One night, while trying to find his way home after an evening of drinking, he found himself near the cave. Not realising where he was, he staggered into the rim of the cave mouth, then turned and ran as if all the hounds of hell were after him. He arrived home stone-cold sober. It was the first time he had been sober for twenty years! He kept promising to tell what he had seen in the cave but could never quite bring himself to do so.

On another Halloween many years later, a shepherd and his flock were passing by the cave and making sure they did not go too near when he heard a burst of music seeming to come from inside the cave. At first it was just a discordant noise but it gradually formed itself into a tune, a tune the like of which the shepherd had never heard before. It stopped and started, changed time and key, got faster and slower ... it was not the music of a sane man.

And then the shepherd saw the musician. He was capering in the cave mouth, his arms sawing at his crwth, his legs each dancing a different rhythm and his head lolling as though it was not attached to his body. The shepherd instantly recognised him though, it was Iolo ap Hugh – Ned Pugh. At that moment the player was sucked back into the cave like smoke being drawn up a chimney and wasn't seen again.

The tune lingered on in the shepherd's memory, although he could never quite bring it to mind enough to whistle or hum it. He moved away soon after that and lived peacefully for many years in another parish between Sycharth and Chirk.

One Sunday evening, as he and the other parishioners sat in the church waiting for the service to begin, they were shocked by a sudden burst of music that seemed to travel under the church from one end of the aisle to the other. The shepherd recognised it as the tune Ned Pugh was playing in the mouth of the cave all those years before. The parson was a keen and able musician and he was able to write the tune down before it was forgotten again, and it is that tune that has come down to us as 'Ffarwel Ned Pugh'. At one time it was one of the best-known tunes in Wales and it is still played occasionally today. It was even arranged by Beethoven with words by a Mrs Hunter!

People still say that, if you go to the cave on Halloween and listen in the cave mouth, you will hear the tune 'Ffarwel Ned Pugh' being played on a crwth as clearly as you can hear the sound of the sea in a seashell. And on certain nights in a leap year a star illuminates the inside of the cave and enables you to see Iolo and his companions leaping and dancing.

I don't think many people dare to try it though.

Are you game?

'In the legend of Iolo ap Hugh, than which no story is more widely known in Wales, the fairy origin of that famous tune 'Ffarwel Ned Pugh' is shown ...' says Wirt Sikes in his book British Goblins *(1880), found on sacred-texts. com. Today both the story and the song are largely forgotten, although the tune is still used for plygain carols. Plygain is a service in the Welsh Church that takes place between three and six on Christmas morning. The carols are often long and ballad like, and include references to the crucifixion as well as birth of Christ. Ned Pugh is, of course, an Anglicisation of Iolo ap Hugh.*

THE FAIRY HARP

In a little cottage in the lane that runs from Dolgellau up to the mountain of Cader Idris, there lived a man called Morgan Preece and his wife Anna. They were poor people who scraped a living from their tiny piece of rough land and by doing any odd jobs that came their way.

Anna loved music and had a fine voice. She sang all the time as she went about her work and when she wasn't working she sang more formally. She sang all the old Welsh songs and accompanied herself on the harp. Anna was quite famous for her music locally and supplemented the family income by playing at musical gatherings at people's houses or in village halls or larger farms when there was a celebration – a wedding, or christening, or sometimes just a party to celebrate someone returning safely from a journey. Anna would entertain them with popular Welsh songs, which they all knew and could join in with, and mix in some of the very ancient ones – the songs that Glasgerion would have known. They loved to hear these but didn't know much about them. She would also mix in a few dance tunes.

Morgan loved music, too. He loved to listen to Anna and his dearest wish was to be able to make music himself. He tried to sing, but his voice sounded like a donkey braying, and when he tried to play on the harp his fingers were so broad and clumsy through years of labouring on the land that he couldn't hit one string at a time, so it sounded awful. Anna always laughed at him when he tried to sing and play but he didn't mind because he loved her and knew that she loved him and that the laughter was just in fun.

'We can't all be good at everything,' he told himself, 'and Anna is hopeless at driving a plough!'

Morgan did mind, though, when his neighbour, Evan Jones, laughed at him. Morgan and Evan did not get on, they never had, although they'd both forgotten why!

One evening, Morgan was sitting alone by the fire waiting for Anna to come back from a music night down in Dolgellau when there was a knock at the door. When he opened it he found three small men in green cloaks, who said politely, 'Sir, we've travelled far and eaten nothing. Could we come in for a warm by the fire and a bite of food?'

'Certainly,' replied Morgan, 'Come in and make yourselves comfortable and I'll see what I can find, although there isn't much until Anna gets back from town.'

So the three small men came in and sat down and Morgan scurried round and dished them up bread and cheese and a glass of beer, and a cake that Anna had baked for Sunday.

When they were rested, the men got up and prepared to leave and their leader turned to Morgan and said, 'You've been very kind to us, Morgan Preece, now we'd like to repay you. Just name anything you'd like and you can have it.'

Now, Morgan didn't take this very seriously, he'd heard stories about wishes that go wrong leaving the recipient with nothing or, worse, a sausage on his nose. He thought the men were joking. A whole list of things from the sublime to the ridiculous spun through his head. And then he settled on one of them. 'Well, Anna always laughs at me when I try to play her harp, so what I'd really like is a harp that I can play,' he said.

'There it is,' said the man, and when Morgan turned to look, there on the table was a small golden harp. 'Bobol anwyl,' said Morgan, crossing himself. 'Where did that come from?' and when he turned round the men had vanished. Morgan picked up the harp, ran his fingers over the strings and, to his amazement, it sounded like music, not the rattle of a tinker's cart. He tried again and out came all the lively dance tunes that he liked so much – and not one wrong note! He was still playing half an hour later when Anna got home.

As soon as she came in and heard the music she dropped her bags, put down her harp and started to dance and kept dancing until she was tired out. 'Stop, stop,' she cried. 'Morgan, please stop playing.'

'You stop dancing,' replied Morgan.

'I can't while you're playing,' gasped Anna, so Morgan stopped playing and Anna sank into an exhausted heap on the rug in front of the hearth. When her heart had stopped racing and she had her breath back, she asked Morgan all about the harp – where had it come from? When had he got it? How had he learned to play it without her knowing? Morgan told her about the three little men but Anna didn't believe a word of it.

Over the next few days, Morgan tried out his harp playing on various friends who came to visit them and, sure enough, as soon as he started to play they had to dance and all the time Morgan played they just had to keep on dancing. Morgan realised that there was magic involved but he didn't want to know too much about it so he just enjoyed the pleasure he got from it without worrying about the consequences. But word spread … You can't keep something like that quiet.

A few days later there was a heavy knock on the door and there stood Morgan's neighbour, Evan Jones. 'What's all this I hear about you playing a harp, Morgan Preece?' he jeered. 'You couldn't play a harp to save your life.' Without a word, Morgan picked up the harp and started to play the fastest, most exhausting dance tune he could think of.

Morgan played and Evan danced and they went on and on until the sweat ran in rivers down Evan's back and his legs began to

tremble with tiredness and he asked Morgan to stop. But he didn't. He kept playing until Evan burst into tears and begged and pleaded with Morgan to stop. Morgan played a few bars more to make Evan really hurt and then put the harp down.

'Oh, I can't play the harp, can't I?' he laughed and then he fell silent as a small, distant voice drifted in through the window: 'Fairy music was not given to you to use in spite,' and when Morgan turned the harp had disappeared.

I can't remember where I found this Welsh story but I used it on a cassette album of stories, Fiddles & Harps & Drums, *way back in 1990.*

DANCE 'TIL YOU DROP

Dancing until you drop is not just something from folk tales and it doesn't need a fairy harp to cause it, it has happened in real life. In June 1374 in Aachen, Germany, 'the populace danced wildly through the streets, screaming of visions and hallucinations, and even continued to writhe and twist after they were too exhausted to stand'. This was dancing mania. There were other occasional cases from the fourteenth to the eighteenth century in Europe. In July 1518, a woman called Frau Troffea began to dance wildly in a street in Strasbourg. She continued to dance non-stop for somewhere between four to six days. Within a week, thirty-four other people had joined her and within a month there were around 400 dancers, most of whom eventually died from a heart attack, a stroke or exhaustion.

This phenomenon was sometimes called St John's Dance or, more commonly, St Vitus' Dance. My Nan used to accuse us kids of having St Vitus' Dance if we fidgeted too much!

Further south, in southern Italy and Sicily, the tarantella is a very energetic dance in 6/8 time performed by couples. Sometimes it develops into a competition between the dancers and the musicians to see who tires first. (Dance 'til you drop!) It is believed to have developed from ancient Greek rituals and beliefs surrounding the bite of a wolf spider that was known as a tarantula (not the same species that we would call a tarantula today). Sustained, energetic dancing was believed to be a cure!

I suppose it is not much different to the twenty-four-hour dance marathons which were popular in the 1950s in dance halls, which would definitely have been out of bounds for members of the various nonconformist churches in Wales who considered dancing one of the worst things you could do! According to Rhys Prydderch in his book *Gemmeu Doethineb* (Gems of Wisdom) 1714, dancing was a worse sin even than marrying a child! There was a well-known joke that if people were going to indulge in illicit sex – perhaps in an alleyway where most people would have done it against the wall, they made sure they laid down in case anyone saw them and thought they were dancing!

For this reason, the Welsh folk dances that bards such as Glasgerion would have known and played became almost extinct by the nineteenth century and were only recovered due to hard work by people including Cecil Sharp and other folk dance collectors.

When I was growing up I remember the criticism of modern dances like jiving or the twist – 'it's like savages in the jungle', our parents or grandparents would say, little knowing that their beloved and respectable waltzes had been called 'riotous and indecent' just a generation or two before because couples danced it face to face and the man had his hand on the lady's waist!

THE HUNCHBACK AND THE FAIRIES

There was a man with a deformed back, a hunchback, as he was called back then. One day he chanced upon the fairies dancing round one of their mounds and they allowed him to accompany them into the mound and join in with the dancing. Because he was so polite, they took pity on him and removed the hump from his back and sent him home as straight and fit as anyone.

A while later another man, a rather brash, overconfident man, was also admitted to the fairies' dance but he was too noisy, too boisterous, and tried to take command and tell them what to do. The fairies didn't like it but didn't do anything until it came to a head when, in a dance, he took the fairy queen round the waist!

This was too much. She ordered them to fetch the hump they had taken from the other man and to put it on this one and he had to live with it for the rest of his life.

Following the rules and conventions of dancers can be very important . No wonder dancing on a Sunday was not allowed until very recently!

A Scottish story.

THE LEGEND OF STANTON DREW

There was a wedding in the small Somerset hamlet of Stanton Drew. It wasn't a grand affair because the couple getting married were just humble country folks. It was a merry affair though, because they had lived in the village all their lives so they knew everyone and everyone knew them and the whole village, from the oldest to the youngest, turned out to wish them luck. After the service in the tiny church they all retired to the hall for food and drink and dancing. Someone had managed to arrange for a fiddler to play and he did a good job of getting everyone up and joining in.

As he played, the fiddler thought about dancing … (It is perfectly possible to play a tune and think about something entirely different at the same time!)

Why do some people love dancing but some find it impossible to do, or embarrassing? Why is it that girls can't wait to get out on to the floor even if it means dancing with each other, while the boys stand around the walls with pints in their hands trying to look cool but only succeeding in looking awkward?

When a good dancer dances with another good dancer it can look as though they are sharing the same body but other couples look as though they are shut into their own little worlds and not even hearing the same music.

Someone would one day say, 'Dancing is a perpendicular expression of a horizontal desire', and that is what the fiddler was aiming for. When the whole room comes together in unison and moves as one, it is the musician's idea of perfection. It doesn't happen every time but when it does it is payment enough and inspires the performer to do it again and again, and hope that it will all fall into place again … this time.

This fiddler was in luck, for this was one of those evenings when it all worked perfectly. Most of the assembly danced every dance and the only ones who didn't were the old folks whose aches and pains made them sit out to have a rest every now and again.

For several hours everyone drank and ate and danced and drank and ate and danced, until those old folks began to say their goodbyes and stumble home or to drop off to sleep there in their chairs with their heads on their plates and spilled ale dripping into their laps.

At that point the newly-weds, accompanied by the fiddler, led their friends out of the hall and down the street in a long, conga-like dance, until they reached a large, level field that gave them a lot more room for some of the more energetic dances young people have always loved.

There they danced in circles and lines, they went forward and back and round and through and dosey-doed and stripped the willow …

As it began to get dark, some paired up and dropped out to disappear behind hedges or into copses. What happened there remained a secret but they returned with satisfied smiles on their faces that they could not hide. As darkness fell, fires were lit and the dancing continued in the gloom. It made it even better, much more atmospheric and mysterious, wilder and more primeval.

But then the fiddler stopped.

It was almost midnight and he had only agreed to play until midnight. In a few minutes it would be Sunday and singing and dancing were not allowed on a Sunday. In fact, not only were they not allowed, they were a serious sin. The fiddler would have no part of it.

The young couple were heartbroken, they were not ready to stop. In fact, they were only just getting going! Their friends felt the same, they wanted to keep dancing all night and still be dancing when the morning sun rose. But the fiddler would not hear of it. They could dance if they liked but he was not going to play. He slung his fiddle on his back and disappeared into the darkness.

'Oh for a musician!' cried the bride. 'Any musician will do, be it the devil himself!'

At that moment they heard distant music gradually getting louder and coming closer and into the midst of the throng came a tall man dressed in black and playing the most thrilling music they'd ever heard. It seemed to compel them to dance, and to dance in a way in which they'd never danced before. If you had heard it you wouldn't have believed he could conjure those sounds from just one simple violin.

The dancers leaped and pranced, they jumped in the air and crawled on the ground, they spun and whirled, sometimes they seemed to be going faster than the eye could see but at other times they sank into a sinuous, snake-like squirm along the ground. They didn't look at the musician, they were too involved with their movements, but if they had they might have noticed a cloven hoof poking out from beneath his cloak, or pointy ears under his cap. When he paused in his playing and licked his lips, his tongue was long and forked. He seemed to be surrounded by a purplish haze and an aroma of rotten eggs.

The dancers didn't tire. The only time they stopped dancing was to couple and rut in twos and threes in full view of everyone else. Then they would dance again. This continued until, with no warning, the sun rose.

At that instant the music ceased and everyone, the dancers and the musician, froze just where they were and turned to stone. No one escaped and none of the young people returned home that day.

As the morning passed, the remaining villagers crept from their homes, met and spoke about the frightening noises they had heard in

the night. They hoped their young people were alright and they went looking for them but they didn't find them. Instead they found a circle of stones looking vaguely like dancers where there had been no stones before, and standing just slightly apart was a tall stone that looked like the musician who had conducted the whole sorry affair.

If you go to Stanton Drew in Somerset you can still see the stones and that proves that my story is true!

The basis of this very well-known story – that stone circles are people who were turned to stone for dancing on Sunday – has been applied to many other stone circles in Britain, and there are over 1,300 of them! The same story is told about stone circles in Germany and Scandinavia, so it's another of those very widespread tales. A song about Stanton Drew was made famous by the folk group the Yetties in the 1970s/80s. It's on YouTube.

Other stone circles, like the Hurlers and the Merry Maidens, both in Cornwall, don't have the whole story about dancers but do have individual stones called 'the piper'. The 'sin' of the Hurlers wasn't dancing but playing sport on a Sunday and Long Meg and Her Daughters are said to be a coven of witches who were turned to stone by the Scottish wizard Michael Scott.

People are still drawn to visit stone circles and they attribute all kinds of powers to them. They are a favourite place for lovers, which might explain the fact that it is often thought impossible to count the stones and get an accurate number – every time another couple makes love within the stones another one is added, one belief says.

JACK AND THE FRIAR

There was a boy called Jack who lived with his father and stepmother.
Jack's real mother had died when he was quite young and since then his
father had married twice more but had not had any more children. Jack's
stepmother hated him; she often wished she could magic him away or he
would get ill and die. It's true he was a bit of a scallywag and sometimes
got up to mischief but he wished no harm on anyone and got on well
enough with most people.

When Jack was old enough to look after himself a bit, his stepmother suggested that they should send him away to work on another
farm. 'To meet new people and see a bit of the world' was her excuse,
but Jack's father said, 'No, not yet, he's not old enough, let's wait a
year or two.' But they did hit upon a compromise: there was a man
who worked on the farm, he slept in the barn and went out every day
with the sheep. They decided that he and Jack should change places,
it would break Jack in gradually, give him some responsibility. When
this was put to Jack, he was all for it. What boy would not like to go
out into the countryside and be his own boss every day.

Next day his stepmother gave Jack some food to last him the day
– it was little enough for a growing lad – and off he went. He took

his dog and the little flock of sheep up on to the hill and let them wander and graze while he sat in the sunshine, looking at the view and daydreaming.

When it got near midday, Jack opened his food and ate a few mouthfuls. Before he'd finished, an old man came along and asked if Jack could spare him a little, and Jack was pleased to give him everything he had left.

When he had eaten, the old man said, 'In return for the food you have given me I can give you three things – just name them, anything you want …'

Jack thought for a minute and said, 'I'd like a little bow to shoot birds with.'

'I will give you,' said the man, 'a bow which will last you your whole life and will never need restringing and, what is more, it will always find its mark. Just point it, draw back the string, and it will always hit the target.' He reached into his bag and drew out a bow, which he handed to Jack, who was overjoyed.

'Now if I just had a pipe – a whistle – then I couldn't be happier,' said Jack.

'I will give you a special pipe,' said the man. 'It is special because when you play it anyone who hears the music must dance, and keep on dancing until you stop playing –' And he reached into his pocket and gave Jack a pipe. 'But I offered you three things,' said the old man, 'what will the third be?'

'I don't need anything more,' said Jack.

'Nothing? Are you sure?'

Jack thought hard. 'Well,' he said, 'At home I have a stepmother who frowns and glares at me as if she'd kill me, and will never offer me a kind word. Whenever she looks at me like that I'd like her to start laughing and keep on laughing until she rolls on the ground and I tell her to stop.'

'Your wish is granted,' said the old man, and went on his way.

Later on, Jack rounded up his flock and set off for home. He played his pipe as he went and the sheep gambolled and skipped along behind him like lambs. The dog joined in too and they got home in record time. Jack stopped playing, put the sheep into the barn, and went into the kitchen. He greeted his father and said that he'd had very little to eat and was ravenously hungry. His father threw him a chicken leg and his stepmother glared at them because it was such a waste. Immediately, for no reason it seemed, she began to giggle and then guffaw, and she shook with laughter and then rolled on the floor and thrashed about and kept on laughing until she was half dead. At last Jack cried, 'Enough!' and she stopped laughing and took herself off to bed, exhausted.

Now, this woman, Jack's stepmother, was being courted by a friar who often came to visit her – usually when Jack's father was away! The next time he came, she told the friar all about how Jack had mocked her and made her laugh until she cried and nearly killed her. She asked the friar to give Jack a good beating to teach him a lesson.

The next day the friar met Jack up on the hill and asked him why he treated his stepmother so badly. 'If you cannot give me an answer then I will have to beat you,' he said.

Jack assured the friar that he meant his stepmother no harm and that she was just imagining that he didn't like her. 'I wish her no more harm than I wish you,' he said, 'and to prove it – look, I have a little bow here, I'll shoot a bird and it will be yours as a gift.'

Jack took his bow and shot at a bird that was flying some distance away. He hit it, of course, and it fell into some brambles. Jack told the friar to go and fetch it and as soon as the friar was in among the brambles he took out his pipe and started to play. The friar dropped the bird and started to dance and the louder Jack played the higher the friar leapt, in among the brambles, until his habit was ripped to shreds and his legs were cut and bleeding. He pleaded with Jack to stop and, at last he did.

The friar ran back to Jack's home, where his beloved, Jack's step-mother, was waiting.

'What has happened to you?' she asked. 'Who did you meet that has set upon you and treated you so badly?'

'I met with your son,' he answered. 'I hope the devil can tame him, because no one else can!'

Then Jack's father came home and was shocked to see the friar there with his habit in rags and his legs covered in bloody scratches. The friar told him what had happened – that Jack had made him dance until he was almost dead, and Jack's father said, 'Well, if that is the case it was very wrong but I will have to see for myself.'

At the usual time, Jack came back from the hill and when his father asked him what he had done to the friar Jack replied, 'Father, I did nothing but play him a tune on my pipe.'

'I would like to hear this tune myself,' said his father.

Jack's stepmother and the friar recoiled in horror, 'No, no, don't let him play!' they shouted.

'If he is going to play then you must tie me to a post so that I can't injure myself,' said the friar.

So they did, and then Jack took out his pipe and began to play. Jack's father and his stepmother began to dance and Jack led them out into the street, where they danced even more wildly. The neighbours, hearing the tune, came out of their houses, some in their night-clothes because many of them had been asleep, and joined in the procession. They danced wildly through the streets and more and more people joined in. You have never seen such wild, frenzied dancing. Jack kept playing until they were begging for mercy and then stopped.

'Well, that's the best fun I've had for seven years!' said Jack's father, but the friar and the stepmother vowed that Jack would be punished.

The following Friday Jack was summoned to appear before the judge, who asked what the charge was and Jack's stepmother scowled at him and declared Jack a witch.

Immediately she started laughing and giggling and howling until Jack stopped her. When they mentioned his pipe and the dancing the judge said, 'I must hear this pipe for myself.' So, of course, Jack played a tune and the whole court erupted into dancing.

After a few minutes, they begged Jack to stop and when he did the judge asked Jack how he would settle the matter. 'Well,' said Jack 'if they promise they will never more do me any harm then I promise I won't do them any harm. There is no reason why we cannot all live in peace.'

And so the matter was settled. The friar and the stepmother went off together to live elsewhere and Jack and his father lived happily in the village. I expect all the other villagers treated Jack with respect from then on and I assume Jack didn't do anything spiteful to them or we would have heard of it. So we can safely say that justice was done and they all lived happily ever after.

This story was unknown to me until I started researching this book. It comes from W. Carew Hazlitt, Tales & Legends of National Origin or Widely Current in England from Early Times, *1899, which is available online.*

JACK HORNER'S MAGIC PIPES

How he met with an old Hermit, who for a Bottle of nappy Ale, gave him an invincible Coat and a Pair of inchanted Pipes, with which he shewed many merry Tricks.

Upon a pleasant holyday,
Jack going to a fair,
And as he passed along the way,
He saw a wonder there.

An aged man sat in a Cave,
Who could not stand nor go,
His head bore blossoms of the grave,
And locks as white as snow,

Strange hollow eyes and wrinkled brow
His nose and chin did meet,
To him Jack Horner made a bow,
With words both soft and sweet.

He call'd to John and thus did say,
Come hither lad to me,
And if thou dost my will obey,
Thou shalt rewarded be:

Bring me a fairing from the town,
At thy own proper cost,
A jug of nappy liquor brown,
Thy labour shan't be lost.

Jack made the Hermit this reply,
Who then sat in his cell,
What's your request I'll not deny,
And so old dad farewel.

At night he being stout and strong,
This Hermit he'd not fail,
But at his back he lug'd along,
A lusty jug of ale:

Which when the Hermit he beheld,
It pleas'd him to the heart;
Out of the same cup he fill'd,
And said, Before we part,

I have a pipe which I'll bestow
Upon you never doubt,
Whoever hears you when you blow,
Shall dance and trump about,

They shan't be able to stand still
While you the Music play,
But after you o'er dale and hill,
They all shall dance the hay.

I have thee a coat likewise,
Invincible I mean,
The which shall so bedim their eyes,
That thou shalt not be seen:

If you with a hundred meet,
When thus you pass along,
Though in the very open street,
Not one of all the throng,

Shall ever see you in the least,
Yet hear the music sound,
And wonder that both man and beast,
Are forced to dance around.

Jack took the Coat and Bagpipes too,
And thankfully did say,
Old Father I will call on you
Whene'er I come this way.

How he serv'd six Fidlers, and as many Pedlers, whom he caused to dance thro' Hedge and Ditch after his Pipes, till they broke all their Glasses and Crowds [crwths].

This Pipe and coat he having got,
He homeward trudg'd with speed,
At length it was his happy Lot
to cross a pleasant Mead:

Where he six Fidlers soon espy'd
a coming from a Fair,
Under their Coats, crowds by their sides,
and many others there:

Amongst the rest six jolly blades,
after those crowders came,
Who on their shoulders carried Crades
with Glasses in the same.

Jack presently his Coat put on,
Which screen'd him from their sight,
And said I'll do the best I can
To plague them all this night.

For Crowders they are Rogues I know
And Crades-men they are worse,
They cousin all where'er they go,
And pick each Lass's purse.

His pipe he then began to play,
The Crowders they did dance,
The Crades-men too as fast as they
Did caper, skip, and prance.

Still Jack play'd up a merry strain,
Both pleasant, loud, and shrill,
So that they danc'd and jump'd amain
Tho' much against their Will:

They cried, this is enchanted Ground,
For why no soul we see,
And yet a pleasant Music sound,
Makes, us dance vehemently.

Jack Horner laugh'd, and piping went
Strait down into a hollow,
These hair brain'd Dancers, by consent
Did after him soon follow,

He led them through Bogs and Sloughs
Nay, likewise Ponds and Ditches,
And in the thorny briar boughs
Poor rogues they tore their Breeches,

Each Fidler lost, or tore his Cloak,
But yet they followed after,
Their crowds were, crack'd their glasses broke,
This was a woeful slaughter.

At length it being something late,
Jack did his piping leave,
They ceased and saw their wretched state,
Which made them sigh and grieve.

This is, said some, Old Nick I know
The author of this evil,
The others cry'd out, if it be so,
He is a merry Devil.

Jack Horner laugh'd and went his Way
And left them in despair,
So that e'er since that very day,
The Fidlers came not there.

'Jack Horner's Magic Pipes'. From The Pleasant History of Jack Horner: containing the witty Tricks and Pleasant Pranks he play'd from his Youth to his riper Years; pleasant and delightful both for Winter and Summer Recreation *by J. Drewry, printer, London, 1790. Available as a free download from various internet sites.*

THE BEE, THE HARP, THE MOUSE AND THE BUM-CLOCK

A long while ago, probably back when your granddad's granddad was still a little boy, in Donegal in Ireland there lived an old widow woman and her son, Jack. They were poor but they were happy and they lived a good life until, at last, hard times came upon them. Their crops failed, plants in their garden withered and they found it very hard to get by. They had no money to buy the things that you can't do without. All they had were three cows, which they loved dearly.

One morning, Jack's mother told him to take the 'branny cow' to market and sell it, so Jack went into the yard and haltered the cow the colour of bran and led it down the road towards the market.

'Make sure you sell it well,' shouted his mother after him.

When Jack got to the town he found a crowd of people standing in the road watching something. They seemed to be enjoying it, so Jack went to have a look.

In the middle of the crowd was a little man with a tiny harp, a bee, a mouse and a bum-clock, which is what the people in Donegal call a cockroach.

The man put them on the ground in front of him and whistled, and straight away the bee began to play the harp and the mouse and the bum-clock got up on their hind legs and started to waltz!

As soon as the music started to play and the mouse and the bum-clock started to dance, the whole crowd joined in, and so did the animals and the hand carts and the pots and pans, and the kettles and skillets and everything in the market. They waltzed around the market place and Jack and the branny cow found themselves joining in as enthusiastically as anyone else.

After a while, the man picked up his pets and put them in his pocket and the animals and the hand carts and the pots and pans, and

the kettles and skillets and everything in the market, including Jack and the branny cow, started to laugh.

The man turned to Jack and said, 'Jack, would you like to be master of these animals?' Jack said he would, but he had no money. 'But you have a fine branny cow,' said the man. 'I will give you the bee and the harp for it.'

'I'd like that,' said Jack, 'but I have a mother at home who is very sad and I have to sell the cow to make her cheer up.'

'Once she sees the bee play the harp she will laugh as she's never laughed before,' said the man, and Jack thought that would be grand so he gave the man the cow and went off home with the bee and the harp in his pocket.

When he got home his mother came out to greet him. 'I see you've sold the cow,' she said. 'Did you get a good deal? Did she make a lot of money?'

'I got a good deal,' said Jack, 'but not money. You wait until you see what I've got in my pocket.' And he took out the bee and the harp and set them down on the ground and whistled. The bee started to play the harp and Jack's mother let out a huge laugh. Then she started to dance and so did Jack and so did the pots and pans, and the kettles and skillets and everything in the house. They jigged and reeled and even the house bounced on its foundations.

After a while Jack picked up the bee and the harp and put them in his pocket and all the dancing stopped – but his mother carried on laughing for quite a while!

When she finally stopped and had got her breath back she was as angry as could be and told Jack he was a stupid fellow and reminded him that they had no food or money and nothing to live on.

'In the morning you must take the black cow to the market and sell her and this time make sure you get a good deal. We need something to live on!'

So, in the morning, Jack went into the yard and haltered the black cow and led it down the road towards the market.

'Don't forget what I told you!' shouted his mother after him.

When Jack got to the town he found a crowd of people standing in the road watching something. They seemed to be enjoying it so Jack went to have a look.

In the middle of the crowd was the little man again with the mouse and the bum-clock.

The man put them on the ground in front of him and whistled and the mouse and the bum-clock got up on their hind legs and started to dance a jig, and as soon as they started to dance the whole crowd joined in, and so did the animals and the hand carts and the pots and pans, and the kettles and skillets and everything in the market. They jigged and reeled and Jack and the black cow found themselves joining in as enthusiastically as anyone else.

After a while the man picked up the mouse and the bum-clock and put them in his pocket and the animals and the hand carts and the pots and pans, and the kettles and skillets and everything in the market, including Jack and the black cow, started to laugh. They laughed and laughed. Then the man turned to Jack and said, 'Jack, would you like to be master of these animals?' Jack said he would, but he had no money and his mother was very downhearted and sad and he had to do something to make her happy again.'

'If she sees this mouse dance she'll be happier than she's ever been before,' said the man.

Jack said again that he had no money. 'But you have a fine black cow. I will give you the mouse for it and then your mother won't be downhearted anymore.'

So Jack exchanged the mouse for the cow and went home to his mother. When she came out to meet him he took the mouse from his pocket with the bee and the harp and he whistled and the bee started to play the harp and the mouse stood up on its hind legs and started to dance a jig and Jack's mother let out a huge laugh. Then she started to dance and so did Jack and so did the pots and pans, and the kettles and skillets and everything in the house. They jigged and reeled and even the house bounced on its foundations again.

After a while Jack picked up the bee and the harp and the mouse and put them in his pocket and all the dancing stopped – but his mother carried on laughing for quite a while!

When she finally stopped and had got her breath back she was as angry as could be and told Jack he was a stupid fellow, a good for nothing.

'In the morning you must take the spotted cow to the market,' she said, 'and make sure you don't come back without a good pocketful of money!'

So, in the morning, Jack went into the yard and haltered the spotted cow and led it down the road towards the market.

'Don't forget what I told you!' shouted his mother after him. 'A pocketful of money!'

When Jack got to the town he found a crowd of people standing in the road watching something. They seemed to be enjoying it so Jack went to have a look.

In the middle of the crowd was the little man with the bum-clock.

The man put it on the ground in front of him and whistled and the bum-clock got up on its hind legs and started to dance – an energetic leaping, rolling dance and as soon as it started the whole crowd joined in, and so did the animals and the hand carts and the pots and pans, and the kettles and skillets and everything in the market. They leaped and rolled and Jack and the black cow found themselves joining in as enthusiastically as anyone else.

After a while the man picked up the bum-clock and put it in his pocket and the animals and the hand carts and the pots and pans, and the kettles and skillets and everything in the market, including Jack and the spotted cow, started to laugh. They laughed and laughed.

The man turned to Jack and said, 'Jack, would you like this bum-clock?' and Jack said he would, but he had no money and his mother was very downhearted and sad and he had to do something to make her happy again.

'Well, there is nothing in the whole world better than this bum-clock to make someone happy. When she sees this bum-clock and the mouse dance to the music of the bee and the harp she'll be happier than she's ever been in her life,' said the man.

Jack said he would love to have them and to make his mother laugh but again, he had no money.

'I would be very willing to swap my bum-clock for your spotted cow,' said the man. 'I would love to make your mother well and happy again.'

So the deal was done and Jack took the bum-clock home and he put it on the floor with the mouse and the bee and the harp and he whistled and the bee began to play the harp and the mouse and the bum-clock got up on their hind legs and started to jive! Jack's mother let out a huge laugh and started to dance and so did Jack and so did the pots and pans, and the kettles and skillets and everything in the house. They jigged and reeled and even the house bounced on its foundations to a good rock 'n' roll beat.

After a while Jack picked them all up and put them in his pocket and all the dancing stopped – but his mother carried on laughing until it turned into sobbing and Jack realised what a fool he was. Now they had no money, no food, no cows. They would starve and it was all Jack's fault.

He wandered off down the road wondering how he could make amends and there he met an old woman. 'I'm surprised you're not off trying for the King of Ireland's daughter,' she said. Jack asked her what she meant.

'Haven't you heard? The King of Ireland has a daughter who hasn't laughed for seven years and he has promised to give her in marriage, along with half the kingdom, to anyone who can get three laughs from her.'

Jack ran back home and fetched the bee, the harp, the mouse and the bum-clock, put them in his pocket and ran off towards the city where the King lived. As soon as he entered the city he was confronted by a row of stakes each with a head on top of it. When he asked what they were he was told they were all the people who had tried to make the princess laugh but failed! Undeterred Jack sent a message to the palace announcing that another person had arrived to try to win her hand.

Before he entered the palace Jack tied the bee to the harp, the harp to the mouse and the mouse to the bum-clock. Then he took the end of the string in his hand and went in. He was shown into a large hall where the court was already assembled. As soon as they saw Jack pulling his little procession behind him they burst out laughing and even the princess was heard to give one loud guffaw. Jack bowed and said, 'Thank you, my Lady. I have already won one third part of you!'

Then Jack whistled and straight away the bee began to play the harp and the mouse and the bum-clock got up on their hind legs and started to waltz! The whole court joined in, and so did the servants and the flunkies and the vases and ornaments, and the empty suits of armour and everything in the palace. They waltzed around the hall as sedately as they were able (which wasn't very!). When Jack stopped the bee playing the whole court burst into peals of laughter and the princess laughed twice as loud as before.

'I now own two parts of you,' said Jack and he started to play again, but however much his little band performed and however much the courtiers danced he was unable to get another laugh from the princess. Jack began to feel very worried and to see his head on a spike, but then the mouse rescued him. It swung round and hit the bum-clock in the mouth with its tail, the bum-clock began to choke and knocked over the harp, which took the bee with it and Jack finished up sitting on the floor. The princess burst into peals of laughter and laughed and laughed. Jack had won her.

He was taken into the inner rooms of the palace and washed and combed and dabbed with perfumes and then dressed in silks and satins. When he met the princess again she said he was the most attractive young man she had ever seen and she would gladly marry him.

Jack sent for his old mother and she came to the wedding, which lasted for nine days and nine nights and each one was grander than the one before.

'All the lords and ladies and gentry of Ireland were at the wedding. I was at it, too, and got brogues, broth and slippers of bread and came jigging home on my head.'

Another story I was unaware of until I started work on this book. Germany-based storyteller Richard Martin pointed me towards it. It is apparently very well known in Ireland, where it is included in many books of fairy tales for children. It comes from Donegal Fairy Stories *by Seumas MacManus, 1900.*

MOSSYCOAT

There was a young woman. She was just getting to the age when young women in her community started to think about marriage. She had started to think about marriage too but had no idea who she wanted to marry. She did know who she did *not* want to marry though – the peddler who came to visit her every time he was in town and brought her presents and made it very clear that one day he wanted her as his wife.

Up until now she had been able to put him off by pretending she didn't understand or by laughing or just by ignoring him, but that was becoming more and more difficult, so she went to her mother for advice. Now her mother was a wise woman, perhaps even a Wise Woman, and she said, 'Don't worry, I have been making you a special coat and it is nearly finished. When it is, you will be able to travel to any place you like in the wink of an eye and to change yourself into anything you like. We just need a bit more time so, next time the peddler comes calling, ask him to get you a present – a dress made of white satin covered with sprigs of gold as big as a man's hand. And it must fit exactly.'

So that is what they did. They thought this would keep the peddler busy for a long while but in just a few weeks he came knocking on the door again and when the girl invited him in he opened his bag and took out a dress made of white satin covered with sprigs of gold as big as a man's hand and when she went to try it on it fitted her exactly.

She asked her mother what to do now and she said, 'Ask him to get you a dress made of fine stuff the colour of all the birds of the air. And it must fit exactly.'

The peddler smiled and went away and returned in an even shorter time with a beautiful dress made of fine stuff the colour of all the birds of the air – and, of course, it fitted exactly.

Again she went to her mother and asked for help. 'Tell him to get you a pair of dancing shoes made of silver. And they must fit exactly.'

Only two or three days passed before the peddler returned and the silver dancing shoes he brought fitted so perfectly that they almost put themselves on the girl's feet and, when she had them on, her feet wanted to dance.

Now her mother said, 'I have almost finished mossycoat, and when I have all your troubles will be over so tell him that you will marry him next week.'

The peddler went on his way with a big smile on his face and the mother worked all that night to finish the coat.

Next day she called her daughter to her and she showed her the coat. It was beautiful but strange, made of moss and embroidered with mystical designs in gold thread but so light that she seemed to be wearing nothing. She told her daughter that from now on she would be called Mossycoat and, when she was wearing it, all her wishes would come true.

So Mossycoat put on the mossycoat, said goodbye to her mother and wished to be far away, and before she knew anything had happened she found herself on a road she had never been on before and a little bit further on was a large mansion.

Mossycoat went up to the front door of the house and knocked and the Lady of the house herself answered. Mossycoat asked if she could have something to eat and drink, and the Lady instantly took a liking to Mossycoat and invited her in. When she had eaten and drunk Mossycoat asked if there was a job she could have in the house. The

Lady asked Mossycoat what she could do and Mossycoat sang a little song she'd learned:

> I can bake and I can brew,
> I can cook an Irish stew,
> Wash a shirt and iron it too
> But I must go home on Sunday
>
> Six days I work with all my might
> To keep the pots and kettles bright
> And hide the cobwebs out of sight
> But I must go home on Sunday.
>
> There is a young man in the town
> One day we'd like to settle down
> And I will have a nice new gown
> When we go out on Sundays.

The Lady liked Mossycoat's song and she was a beautiful-looking young woman, so she said they were in need of an undercook and Mossycoat would be just right for that. Then she took her down to the kitchen and introduced her to the cook and the other servants as the new undercook. The other servants were not very pleased with this idea. As undercook she would be over them and they did not want to take orders from some strange young woman they knew nothing about, so instead of undercook Mossycoat became the skivvy, the lowest, most menial servant in the kitchen. She had to get up first to light the fires so that there was hot water for the other servants and she was given all the dirtiest pans to clean and it was her job to keep the floors swept and the bins emptied. If she did not do it well enough (and even when she did) one or other of the servants would hit her pop, pop, pop on the head with a skillet.

The Master and Mistress of the house did not seem to notice because it did not happen when they were around but they kept an interested eye on Mossycoat. And so did their son, a young gentleman of about Mossycoat's own age who rather fancied the new servant.

I don't really know why Mossycoat put up with it and continued working there in the kitchen but she did, until one day everyone was bursting with excitement. There was going to be a ball. It would last for three days and would be the largest, most important ball there had been in the county for many years. It was all the servants could talk about and they all wished they were going and told each other about what it would be like and what they would do if they were there. They fantasised about all the glamorous dresses and giggled about the handsome young men and each one thought that, if they could only be there, they would catch a fine husband. Among all this frivolity they all turned on Mossycoat and teased her about what would happen if she went with her dirty face and greasy clothes and, just to rub it in, they always finished by hitting her pop, pop, pop on the head with a skillet.

Then Mossycoat was summoned upstairs to meet the Master and Mistress. They said the Young Master would like to invite Mossycoat to go with him to the ball as his guest. Mossycoat declined, she said she couldn't possibly because she'd make all the seats greasy and if any young man danced with her she'd spoil his clothes and the dresses of the ladies who passed too near. The Master and Mistress, and especially the Young Master, tried to make her change her mind but she wouldn't.

When she came back down to the kitchen, the servants all gathered round and asked her why she'd been summoned. Was she being sacked? Was she in trouble?

When she told them that she had been invited to accompany the Young Master to the ball they called her a liar and pushed her and pinched her and hit her pop, pop, pop on the head with a skillet.

The first day of the ball was a huge success and the Master and Mistress and the Young Master had a grand time. Servants have a special gossip pipeline; word travels many miles without anyone seeming to do anything, and the next morning they were all talking about it with as much knowledge and authority as if they had been there. Then they teased Mossycoat and said it would have been funny if she had gone in her rags and with her dirty face! And they hit her pop, pop, pop on the head with a skillet.

So Mossycoat decided she would go to the ball that night.

As soon as the Master and Mistress and the Young Master left in their carriage, Mossycoat put all the servants into a magic sleep, wished that she was clean and coiffured, put on the dress of white satin covered with sprigs of gold as big as a man's hand and her silver dancing shoes, and wished to be at the ball.

And she was. No one was aware of her arrival but, as she stood watching the proceedings, they gradually noticed her. 'Who is that beautiful young stranger?' they asked each other. When the dancing started all the young men asked her to dance but she refused them all. This made her even more enticing. The older people engaged her in conversation but, although she was polite, she would tell them nothing. At last, when the Last Waltz was announced, Mossycoat agreed to dance with the Young Master. She was a fine dancer and everyone watched the couple until, a few bars before the dance ended, Mossycoat wished to be home, and was. The Young Master was left with empty arms looking, and feeling, silly!

Mossycoat quickly magicked her old rags back on, dirtied her face and hands, and woke up the other servants with threats that if they offended her she would tell their master and mistress about them spending the whole evening asleep.

The next day the whole county was abuzz with talk about the young woman who had been at the ball and had danced so beautifully and then mysteriously disappeared. They wondered whether she would come again that night. The servants in Mossycoat's kitchen could talk about nothing else and teased Mossycoat about it but as soon as one of them picked up a skillet to hit her pop, pop, pop on the head she reminded them that they had all been asleep when they should have been working and that she could report them.

That night the same thing happened. Mossycoat sent the servants to sleep, put on the dress the colour of all the birds of the air and the silver dancing shoes and went to the ball. Everyone was waiting for her but they didn't see her arrive – they were looking for a carriage and horses – and again Mossycoat would not dance until the very last dance. She did talk to her Master and Mistress, who did not recognise her though, and when they asked her where she came from she told them she lived in a house where they hit her pop, pop, pop on the head with a skillet. This puzzled them and made her even more interesting.

By now the Young Master was hopelessly in love with the mysterious young lady and he was not going to let her escape from him this time. As the dance finished, he kept tight hold of her and felt her rise into the air but she turned into mist and he could not prevent her from disappearing. He did, however, have hold of one of her silver dancing shoes.

The next day he was dying for love and the doctors said that he could only be saved by marrying the young woman from the ball so word was sent out that he would marry whoever could wear the silver dancing shoe.

All the fine young Gentlewomen came to try the shoe but it would fit none of them. Then all the daughters of farmers and businessmen were brought without any luck. All the girls from the town came and eventually even the servants from the kitchen, but none of them could wear the shoe.

'Is there no one else?' they asked desperately.

'Well, there is Mossycoat. She's hiding in the kitchen.'

'Bring her.'

Mossycoat was brought and the shoe slipped on her foot perfectly. Then the Young Master rose from his bed and went down on one knee in order to propose to her.

'Wait,' she said and disappeared back to her room. In the wink of an eye she returned wearing the dress of white satin covered with sprigs of gold as big as a man's hand. Everyone gasped in amazement and the young master tried to take her in his arms.

'Wait,' she said again and went back to her room and reappeared in the dress the colour of all the birds of the air. This time she did not stop the young master from kissing her and she agreed to his proposal of marriage.

When everything had calmed down, she explained to the Master and Mistress all about her magic coat and how she'd been able to go to the ball. The one thing they couldn't understand was about her being hit pop, pop, pop on the head with a skillet and when she told them that it was the servants in their kitchen who did that they turned them out of doors and the dogs were set upon them and they were never seen again.

Mossycoat and the Young Master were married and had a large family and lived happily ever after.

Mossycoat is one of the most famous English folk tales. It was one of the first stories I learned when I started telling tales nearly forty years ago. It is, of course, a variant of Cinderella, Catskin, Cap o' Rushes etc., a story that is found all over the world. Mossycoat comes from from Folk Tales of England, *edited by Katherine Briggs and Ruth Tongue, 1965, where it appears in Gypsy dialect.*

The little song I have Mossycoat sing I collected from Bedfordshire singer Margery (Mum) Johnstone (born 1901), who learned it from her granny when she was a little girl.

THE FROG AT THE WELL

Kissing a frog is one of the best-known folk tale motifs there is and everyone knows it. It has become a common figure of speech. Storytellers will tell you that it was hearing a Scottish version of this tale that inspired the Brothers Grimm to start their collection!

One morning a young woman took her jug and went down to the well to fetch some water, but when she got there she found the well had gone dry – no water. So she sat on the edge of the well and started to cry. Now, any of you modern, capable, educated women reading this wouldn't behave in that way would you? You'd know how to get the well unblocked or would call the plumber or phone for a delivery of bottled water from a supermarket, or something … but none of those options were open to her, so she just sat on the edge of the well, and cried …

As she was sitting there, crying, a frog came plopping along the path towards her and when it got there it said, 'Hello, why are you crying?'

'Because the well's gone dry and there's no water.'

'Well, if you marry me you can have all the water you want,' said the frog.

She didn't fancy marrying a frog … she didn't know anyone who had married a frog, none of her friends had married frogs … but she couldn't really think of any good reason not to, so she said, 'Alright', and when she looked the well was full of water. Without giving the frog another thought, she filled her jug and went home.

That night, when she and her mother were getting ready for bed, there was a sudden commotion outside the door and someone started singing:

Open the door, my hinny, my heart
Open the door, my deary,
Remember the promise that you and I made
Down in the meadow so early.

'Who's that singing outside the door?' asked the mother.

'Oh, it must be that old frog I met down by the well this morning.'

'Well, let him in, it's cold out there.'

So the girl let him in and he sat down by the fire and got warm and then he sang:

Give me my supper, my hinny, my heart
Give me my supper, my deary,
Remember the promise that you and I made
Down in the meadow so early.'

And the mother sent the daughter into the kitchen to bring the frog some supper. She wasn't quite sure what a frog would want for supper so she piled up a tray with all kinds of things and brought it back and the frog ate the lot. Then it licked its lips and burped and sang:

Put me to bed, my hinny, my heart
Put me to bed, my deary,
Remember the promise that you and I made
Down in the meadow so early.

So the girl went into the bedroom and did all the things you do to a visitor's bed – she puffed up the pillows and tucked in the sheets and smoothed out the blankets and the frog jumped into bed and then he looked at her and sang:

> Jump into bed, my hinny, my heart
> Jump into bed, my deary,
> Remember the promise that you and I made
> Down in the meadow so early.

Now she didn't much fancy getting into bed with a frog but her mother had made her do everything else so she didn't think it was worth arguing. So she got into bed and lay down on one side while the frog was the other side and she made sure there was a big space down the middle of the bed between them. But the frog looked at her and sang:

> Give me a kiss, my hinny, my heart
> Give me a kiss, my deary,
> Remember the promise that you and I made
> Down in the meadow so early.

So she screwed up her eyes and she screwed up her lips and she screwed up her courage and she screwed up everything else which she could think of she could possibly screw up, and she leaned over and gave the frog a quick, little peck on the lips.

And when she opened her eyes … I'm sure you have guessed, instead of a frog there was the most handsome young man she'd seen in her whole life and he said, 'Thank you, you've saved me from a wicked enchantment …' and what happened next I will leave to your imagination!

A north of England version of a very well-known story reprinted from my book Where Dragons Soar and other Animal Folk Tales of the British Isles, *The History Press, 2016.*

KATE CRACKERNUTS

Once upon a time there was a man, a widower, who had a daughter, Ann. There was also a woman, a widow, who had a daughter, Kate. In those times it was not practical or socially acceptable to be a 'one-parent family', so the man and the woman married. Ann and Kate, now stepsisters, got on well together, they loved each other and were good friends, although they were very different. Ann was beautiful and gentle, while Kate was a tomboy.

Kate's mother was jealous of Ann – why should she be more beautiful and ladylike than her own daughter? She was scared that it would give her a better chance of finding a good husband when that time came, and it would not be too many years.

She decided she would spoil Ann's beauty, so she went to an old woman who lived nearby who kept hens. As well as being the hen-wife, she also had a reputation as a witch; not one of those silly witches who wear pointy hats and ride around on broomsticks but a much more practical sort of witch who made medicines and potions to either kill or cure you! The hen-wife told the woman she would help and to send Ann to her the next morning – *before she has had anything to eat.*

So, next morning, the woman called Ann and asked her to quickly run to the hen-wife and bring back some eggs. 'Go quickly, now, before you have your breakfast,' she said. And Ann did. But as she was going through the kitchen she saw a stale crust lying on the table and took it to eat as she went along.

When she reached the hen-wife's house, she asked for the eggs and the hen-wife told her to lift the lid and look in a large pot. She did so but saw nothing.

'Take these eggs and go home and tell your mother to lock her larder door better!' she said.

The next morning the woman sent Ann to the hen-wife again and this time she made sure she left without eating anything, but as she went along the lane she saw some workers picking peas and she begged a handful of them. Again the hen-wife told Ann to look in the pot and, again, nothing happened.

The hen-wife was furious. Tell your mother, 'The pot won't boil if the fire's out,' she said. Ann didn't understand but when she got home she gave her mother the message.

The third morning the woman took Ann to the hen-wife herself to make sure that she ate nothing at all and when she lifted the lid and looked in her face began to change. It began to melt and lost its features and grew long and white, her hair shrivelled up until it was white and curly, her eye lashes curled up and all in all she began to look like a sheep!

At this the woman was satisfied and took Ann home.

Kate was horrified when she saw Ann but did her best to comfort her. 'We won't let this come between us,' she said. 'We'll go away and seek our fortune.' She found a fine lace cloth and wrapped it round Ann's face like a veil and off they went. If they met anyone Kate explained that her sister was sick.

At length they came to a castle and asked for a night's lodging. The king of this castle had two sons and one of them was wasting away with a strange sickness. No one could explain it and, even stranger, anyone who sat up with him at night mysteriously disappeared and

was never seen again. The king had offered a purse full of silver coins to anyone who could sit up with him and explain what happened. Kate, being a brave girl, volunteered to try.

All went well, meaning nothing happened at all, until the clock struck midnight. Then the prince rose and dressed himself, slipped downstairs to the stable, saddled his horse, called his hound, and galloped off; but Kate, as quick as lightning, jumped on to the horse behind him, and he seemed not to notice a thing.

They rode and rode and as they went Kate picked nuts from the bushes they passed. At last they came to a round, green hill. The prince reined in his horse and called out, 'Open, and admit the young prince and his horse and his hound.'

'With his Lady behind him!' Kate quickly added.

Immediately a door in the side of the hill opened and they rode into a huge hall, brightly lit and full of gaily clad people all dancing. Kate realised they were fairies. She hid behind a door as the fairies gathered round the prince and he danced with them each in turn until he was exhausted. Then he laid on a couch while they fanned him and his strength returned. Then he danced again and so on, over and over. At last they heard the cocks begin to crow and the prince leapt on his horse, with Kate behind him, and galloped back to his home and his bed where he lay ill and exhausted.

When the king came to visit them he found the prince asleep and Kate sitting by the fire cracking nuts. She said that the prince had had a good night and she would sit up with him again if the king gave her a purse of gold.

The next night the same thing happened, but instead of watching the prince dance Kate watched to see what the other fairies were doing. She saw a baby fairy playing with a wand and heard one of the fairies say, 'Just three strokes from that wand would make Kate's sister as fair as ever she was.' So Kate rolled nuts towards the baby, which was so fascinated that it dropped the wand and chased after them. Kate picked up the wand and hid it in her pocket. At cock crow they galloped home again and Kate immediately touched Ann three times with the wand and her face returned to its own form, as beautiful as ever it had been.

Kate said that she would stay with the prince for another night on condition that she could marry him and the king agreed. Everything went as before but this time the baby fairy was playing with a small bird. Kate heard the other fairies say that three mouthfuls of this bird would cure the sick prince – he would be his old self again, so she rolled the nuts until the baby dropped the bird to pick them up. Kate seized it and later, as they rode home, she plucked it. As soon as she was back in the prince's room she cooked the bird and the prince was awoken by the smell.

'If only I could have a bite of that bird,' he said, and Kate gave him a mouthful. The prince pulled himself up in the bed and leaned on his elbow. 'Mmm, if I could have another bite,' he said. Kate gave him another mouthful and he sat up in bed. 'I would really like a third bite of that bird,' he said and when Kate gave him another mouthful he jumped out of bed, dressed himself and was perfectly well. When the king came in next morning he found Kate and his son sitting by the fire happily cracking nuts. Then the other son met Ann and they fell in love and pretty soon both couples married.

'So the sick son married the well sister, and the well son married the sick sister, and they all lived happy and died happy and never drank out of a dry cappy.'

Well known in the storytelling revival, this is one of the classic tales from Joseph Jacobs' English Fairy Tales, 1890, although he says in his notes that his source was so corrupt that he had to largely rewrite it. With that in mind, I have also rewritten it a bit more than some of the others.

ORANGE AND LEMON

Once upon a time there were two little girls. One was called Orange and the other was called Lemon, although their names are irrelevant to the story; they could just as well have been Mary and Jane, but Orange and Lemon they were so Orange and Lemon they will remain.

Now their mother liked Lemon best and father liked Orange best, so when he was out at work Orange was given all the difficult, dirty chores to do.

One day Mother called Orange and said, 'I want you to go down to the well and fetch a jug of water,' and then she said all the things mothers always say: 'and you must go straight there and back and don't get playing with your friends and don't get your dress dirty and whatever you don't break the jug *or I will kill you!*' (Perhaps mothers don't usually say that last bit ...)

You can guess what happened. Orange took the jug, went out of the door, and before she'd even got to the end of the garden path she fell over and broke the jug. She was terrified and didn't dare go back in and tell her mother what she'd done so she hung around in the garden and then tried to sneak in without being seen. But she was.

'Where have you been?' shouted mother. 'Where's my jug? You haven't broken it, have you?' And Orange had to admit that she had.

Mother went very quiet and had that look on her face that Orange knew meant she was in big trouble.

'Light the fire,' said mother. So Orange lit the fire.

'Put the pan on to boil.' So Orange put water in the pan and placed it on the fire.

'Fetch the chopping block.' Orange fetched the chopping block.

'Fetch the axe.' Orange fetched the axe.

And mother laid Orange over the chopping block and cut off her head and put it in the pan to cook! Then she told Lemon to take Orange's body down into the garden and bury it.

A few hours later father came home from work. 'Where's Orange?' he asked.

'She's off doing some errands,' said mother.

'What's for tea?'

'Sheep's head stew.'

And mother dished up the stew and father ate it and it was delicious. When he'd finished he sat down in his armchair in front of the fire and dozed off to sleep.

Meanwhile, Orange's spirit had flown off to the shoemaker's shop and it sat on the shoemaker's chimney pot and sang down the chimney:

My mother chopped my head off,
My father picked my bones,
My little sister buried me
Beneath cold marble stones.

And the shoemaker said, 'If you will sing that again I'll give you a fine pair of leather boots.' So Orange sang it again:

My mother chopped my head off,
My father picked my bones,

My little sister buried me
Beneath cold marble stones.

And the shoemaker gave her a fine pair of leather boots.

Then she flew off to the jeweller's shop and it sat on the jeweller's chimney pot and sang down the chimney:

My mother chopped my head off,
My father picked my bones,
My little sister buried me
Beneath cold marble stones.

And the jeweller said, 'If you will sing that again I'll give you a fine gold watch.'

So she sang it again:

My mother chopped my head off,
My father picked my bones,
My little sister buried me
Beneath cold marble stones.

And the jeweller gave her a fine gold pocket watch.

Then Orange flew off to the stonemason's shop and sang down the chimney:

My mother chopped my head off,
My father picked my bones,
My little sister buried me
Beneath cold marble stones.

And the stonemason said, 'If you will sing that again I'll give you a block of marble as big as your head.'

So she did and he did.

Then, with the fine leather boots, the gold pocket watch and the block of marble as big as her head, Orange went home and sat on her own rooftop and sang down the chimney

Sister, sister come to me
And see what I have got for thee.

And Lemon went to the fireplace and reached up and Orange lowered down the fine pair of leather boots, which fitted her exactly.

Then Orange sang:

Father, father come to me
And see what I have got for thee.

And when father got to the fireplace, Orange lowered down the chimney the gold pocket watch and he was thrilled because he'd never had a watch before.

Then Orange sang down the chimney:

Mother, mother come to me
And see what I have got for thee.

And mother didn't just go to the fireplace but she went right into the fireplace and reached up, eager to see what gift Orange had for her.

And Orange threw down the block of marble as big as her head with all her might and smashed her mother to smithereens!

A very well-known tale with many versions from all over Europe – the Grimms' 'The Juniper Tree' is perhaps the most widely known. British versions have been collected by Baring-Gould and Addy, among others. It is/was particularly popular among the travellers of Scotland, where it is usually known as 'Applie and Orangie'.

Many years ago I used to tell this to older children in schools. I don't know whether I would be allowed to now …? Definitely not PC!

HANGMAN, OR THE PRICKLY BUSH

Oh, the prickly bush, the prickly bush
That pricks my heart full sore;
If ever I get out of the prickly bush
I'll never get in him any more …

There were two little girls, they might have been twins or they might
not, but they were very close together in age and in looks, but very different in character. Everyone loved them – particularly the Magician.

One day he came to their house with a present for each of them
– exactly the same thing for both. It was a beautiful golden ball in a
polished wooden box lined with velvet with a lock and a clasp on
the front.

But along with the present came a warning: if you ever lose your
golden ball you will be taken away and hanged!

They both loved their presents in their own, very different, ways.

One girl thought it was so precious that she looked at it and then
locked the ball in its box, hid the box away in the back of a cupboard,

locked the cupboard, hid the key and moved her bed so that it stopped the cupboard door from opening. She was not going to risk losing her golden ball!

But the other sister loved the ball as an object. She loved its size and its weight, the coolness of its surface and the way it reflected the light. She loved to roll it from hand to hand and to toss it in the air and catch it. She'd do this for ages and while she did so she'd go off into a daydream and not think about anything at all.

One morning she was walking through the park and as she went she tossed her ball up and caught it … and tossed her ball up and caught it … and wandered along not really looking or thinking where she was going, and she tossed her ball up and caught it … and tossed her ball up and caught it … and by now she was near the edge of the park and she tossed her ball up and … it went over the railings.

These railings were very close together so she couldn't squeeze through them. They were very high so she couldn't climb over. She couldn't dig underneath them and they stretched for miles so she couldn't go round them. Inside the railings was a house where a witch lived.

She could see her ball lying just inside the railings, so she tried reaching her arm through but it wasn't long enough; she tried poking it with sticks but although she could touch the ball she couldn't move it. In the end she gave up and went home. And they were waiting for her and they took her off and locked her in a dungeon while, outside, they built a gallows on which to hang her.

She was in the dungeon for three days and three nights and on the following morning she heard the footsteps of many people as they made their way to the town square, and then the voices of the crowd as they gathered to watch the execution – for in those days a public hanging was still a spectacle that everyone wanted to attend. Not only was there the hanging but there was the chance to see old friends, to buy souvenirs, to hear singers and poets and storytellers telling of the crimes of the person who was to be hanged, and to sample the wares of various food and drink sellers.

Then there were voices outside the cell and the door opened. In came several guards, the mayor, the hangman and a priest. They tied her hands and led her out of the building, up the steps and on to the scaffold.

The crowd drew in their breath and then moved forward in order to see better. A hush of expectation hung over the square. She wasn't a notorious murderer and she hadn't done any really terrible crime, so they didn't throw things or yell obscenities at her, they just waited.

The hangman went through his routine of measuring the rope and checking the knot and making sure that the trap would open properly, and then they were ready.

But at that moment there was a movement at the back of the crowd and her father came riding up.

She sang:

Hangman, slack your rope,
Slack it for a while,
I think I see my father coming
Riding many a mile.
O father have you brought me hope?
Or have you paid my fee?
Or have you come to see me hanging
On the gallows tree?

I have not brought you hope.
And I have not paid your fee.
Yes, I have come to see you hanging
On the gallows tree

And he climbed down from his horse and joined the crowd, who sighed and shuffled. The hangman tugged the rope again and the mayor started to read the charges against her. And then, there was another movement at the back of the crowd – another rider on a horse.

Hangman, slack your rope,
Slack it for a while,
I think I see my mother coming
Riding many a mile.
O mother have you brought me hope?
Or have you paid my fee?
Or have you come to see me hanging
On the gallows tree?

I have not brought you hope.
And I have not paid your fee.
Yes, I have come to see you hanging
On the gallows tree

And she dismounted and joined her husband in the crowd. The priest opened his prayer book and read the passages appropriate for a public execution and the hangman readied the blindfold. Then …

Hangman, slack your rope,
Slack it for a while,
I think I see my sister coming
Riding many a mile.
O sister have you brought me hope?
Or have you paid my fee?
Or have you come to see me hanging
From the gallows tree?

I have not brought you hope.
And I have not paid your fee.
Yes, I have come to see you hanging
From the gallows tree.

Her sister didn't just say this but she said it with a sneer. I'm sure you know the way sisters talk to each other when one of them has done something wrong and the other is feeling smug and self-righteous? It wasn't quite a thumb on the nose and waving fingers and 'Nah, nah-ne, nah, nah …' but it was almost.

'If you had been sensible like me and looked after your golden ball and not gone throwing it about in the park then you wouldn't be where you are now. It's all your own fault,' her tone suggested …

And, like her parents, she joined the audience to watch the event.

The hangman shook the blindfold but she said that she did not want to be blindfolded, she wanted to continue to watch the crowd for she was sure that she would be saved.

All was ready. The crowd was restive. The mayor and the priest and above all the hangman were ready (he was very ready because he wouldn't get paid overtime!). He put the noose round her neck, grasped the lever that sprung the trap when …

Hangman, slack your rope,
Slack it for a while,
I think I see my true love coming
Riding many a mile.
O true-love have you brought me hope?
True love have you paid my fee?
Or have you come to see me hanging
From the gallows tree?

Yes, I have brought you hope.
And I have paid your fee.
No, I've not come to see you hanging
From the gallows tree.

And he urged his horse through the crowd and up to the scaffold. Then he reached behind him into his saddle bag and pulled out the golden ball, which he presented to the mayor.

A huge cheer went up from the crowd because, although they were happy enough to watch the execution, they were even happier that true love had won the day and she had been saved.

The hangman released the noose, she sprang on to the back of her true love's horse and they spurred their way through the crowd and away. They came to his house, where they prepared to live happily ever after …

But before they did that she needed to know – how he had known that she was in the dungeon and going to be hanged? And how he had managed to get her golden ball back and be there to rescue her?

Word had reached him, he said, and he knew that he had to save her so he went to the railings where she had lost her golden ball and he couldn't get through the railings, or over the railings, or under, or round the railings, but he had to do something. He also tried poking with his sword and his spear and all kinds of other things but he could not get the ball. So, in the end, with a super-human effort he managed to scramble to the top, and as he perched there, getting his breath back, the old witch came out and told him, 'If you want the golden ball you'll have to agree to spend three nights in the haunted house.'

He did agree, of course.

On the first night he was upstairs in a room in the house and he could hear all the ghosts and goblins playing around in the yard when, with huge steps that shook the house, he heard a giant coming up the stairs. He hid behind the door before the giant came in. Giants might be very big but they are not very bright and this one took a quick look round the room, didn't see the man hiding behind the door, and went over to the window. He stuck his head out and called down, 'I thought you said there was an Englishman up here …'. While he had his head out of the window, our hero sneaked out from behind the door, took his sword and chopped off the giant's head, which fell down into the yard. Then he took the giant's body and rammed it up the chimney.

The second night was quite similar. Another giant came stomping up the stairs but this time he didn't hide behind the door, he just stood in the middle of the room and as the giant came into the room he swung his sword and cut the giant clean in half. The legs continued across the room and out of the window and, again, he stuffed the other half up the chimney.

For some reason (I don't know why but it does allow me to get in an excruciatingly bad joke), the third night was a bit different. He was lying on the bed and he could hear all the ghosts and goblins playing around under it. They were rolling the golden ball backwards and forwards and round and round. He could hear it trundling from the head to the foot and back again and from one side to the other … Every now and again an arm or a leg would poke out from under the bed and with his sword he'd cut it off so that, pretty soon the ghosts and goblins were all quite *'armless* and he was able to take the ball, jump on his horse and ride to the town square just in time to rescue her, as you have already heard.

> Oh, the prickly bush, the prickly bush
> That pricks my heart full sore;
> Now I've got out of the prickly bush
> I'll never get in him any more …

A story I have told and a song I've sung for several decades. 'The Maid Freed from the Gallows' or 'The Prickly Bush' (Child Ballad #95) has been sung by many British folk singers including A.L. Lloyd, Bert Jansch and Bellowhead; many American singers like Jean Ritchie and Peter, Paul & Mary; and, under the title 'The Gallis Pole', by American Blues singer Leadbelly and 'Gallows Pole' by rock band Led Zeppelin. I recorded the song on my 1982 LP Rambling Robin, *before I'd ever thought of telling stories. All those are the stand-alone song though. It makes much more sense when combined with the story, which comes from Joseph Jacobs'* More English Fairy Tales, *1894. I included a shorter, less gruesome, version in* Derbyshire Folk Tales.

TOM TIT TOT

Once upon a time there was a woman who baked five pies. When they came out of the oven they were that overbaked, the crusts were too hard to eat. So she says to her daughter: 'Daughter,' says she, 'put them there pies on the shelf, and leave them there for a little while, and they'll come again.' (She meant the crust would get softer.)

But the girl, she says to herself: 'Well, if they'll come again, I'll eat them now,' and she set to work and ate them all, first and last.

Well, come supper-time the woman said: 'Go and get one of them there pies. I dare say they will have come again by now.'

The girl went and she looked, and there was nothing but the empty dishes. So back she came and says, 'No, they haven't come again.'

'Not one of them?' says the mother.

'Not one of them,' says she.

'Well, come again, or not come again,' said the woman, 'I'll have one for supper.'

'But you can't, if they haven't come,' said the girl.

'But I can,' says she. 'Go and bring the best of them.'

'Best or worst,' says the girl, 'I've eaten them all, and you can't have one till they've come again.'

Well, the woman she was done, and she took her spinning to the door to spin, and as she span she sang:

> My daughter she ate five pies today, five pies today, five pies today.
> My daughter she ate five pies today, five pies today.

The king was coming down the street, and he heard her sing, but what she sang he couldn't quite hear, so he stopped and said, 'What was that you were singing, my good woman?'

The woman was ashamed to let him hear what her daughter had been doing, so instead she sang:

> My daughter she spun five skeins today, five skeins today, five skeins today.
> My daughter she spun five skeins today, five skeins today.

'Stars o' mine!' said the king, 'I never heard tell of anyone that could do that.' Then he said, 'Look you here, I want a wife, and I'll marry your daughter. But look you here,' says he, 'eleven months out of the year she shall have all she likes to eat, and all the gowns she likes to buy, and all the company she likes to keep; but the last month of the year she'll have to spin five skeins every day, and if she doesn't I shall kill her.'

'All right,' says the woman; for she thought what a grand marriage that was. And as for the five skeins, when the time came, there'd be plenty of ways of getting out of it, and likeliest he'd have forgotten all about it.

Well, so they were married. And for eleven months the girl had all she liked to eat, and all the gowns she liked to buy, and all the company she liked to keep.

But when the end of the eleven months were drawing near she began to think about the skeins and to wonder if he had them in mind. But not one word did he say about them, and she thought he'd wholly forgotten them.

However, on the last day of the last month he took her to a room she'd never set eyes on before. There was nothing in it but a spinning wheel and a stool. And he says, 'Now, my dear, here you'll be shut in tomorrow with some victuals and some flax, and if you haven't spun five skeins by the night, your head will come off.'

And away he went about his business.

Well, she was that frightened. She'd always been such a hopeless girl she didn't even know how to spin, and what was she to do tomorrow with no one to come to help her? She sat down on a stool in the kitchen and, law, how she did cry!

However, all of a sudden she heard a sort of a knocking low down on the door. She upped and opened it, and what should she see but a small little black thing with a long tail.

It looked up at her right curious, and said, 'What are you a-crying for?'

'What's it to you?' says she.

'Never you mind,' it said, 'but tell me what you're crying for.'

'It won't do me no good if I do,' says she.

'You don't know that,' it said, and twirled its tail round.

'Well,' says she, 'it won't do any harm if it doesn't do any good,' and she upped and told about the pies, and the skeins, and everything.

'This is what I'll do,' says the little black thing. 'I'll come to your window every morning and take the flax and bring it back spun at night.'

'What's your pay?' says she.

It looked out of the corner of its eyes, and said, 'I'll give you three chances every night to guess my name, and if you haven't guessed it before the month's up you shall be mine.'

Well, she thought, she'd be sure to guess its name before the month was up. 'All right,' says she, 'I agree.'

'All right,' it says, and law, how it twirled its tail.

Well, the next day her husband took her into the room, and there was the flax and the day's food.

'Now, there's the flax,' says he, 'and if it isn't spun up this night, off goes your head.' And then he went out and locked the door.

He'd hardly gone, when there was a knocking against the window.

She upped and she opened it, and there sure enough was the little old thing sitting on the ledge.

'Where's the flax?' says he.

'Here it is,' says she. And she gave it to him.

Well, come the evening a knocking came again to the window. She upped and she opened it, and there was the little old thing with five skeins of spun flax on his arm.

'Here it is,' says he, and he gave it to her.

'Now, what's my name?' says he.

'Is it Bill?' says she.

'Nooo, that ain't,' says he, and he twirled his tail.

'Is it Ned?' says she.

'Nooo, that ain't,' says he, and he twirled his tail.

'Well, is it Mark?' says she.

'Nooo, that ain't,' says he, and he twirled his tail harder, and away he flew.

Well, when her husband came in there were the five skeins all spun ready for him.

'I see I shan't have to kill you tonight, my dear,' says he; 'you'll have your food and your flax in the morning,' says he, and away he goes.

Well, every day the flax and the food were brought, and every day that there little black imp came mornings and evenings. And all day the girl sat trying to think of names to say to it when it came at night. But she never hit on the right one. And as it got towards the end of the month the imp began to look so full of malice, and it twirled its tail faster and faster each time she gave a guess.

At last it came to the last day but one. The imp came at night along with the five skeins, and it said, 'What, ain't you got my name yet?'

'Is it Nicodemus?' says she.

'Nooo, 't ain't,' it says.

'Is it Sammle?' says she.

'Nooo, 't ain't,' it says.

'Well, is it Methusalem?' says she.

'Nooo, 't ain't that neither,' it says.

Then it looks at her with its eyes like a coal of fire, and it says, 'Woman, there's only tomorrow night, and then you'll be mine!' And away it flew.

Well, she felt that was horrid. However, she heard the king coming along the passage. In he came, and when he sees the five skeins, he says, 'Well, my dear,' says he. 'I don't see but that you'll have your skeins ready tomorrow night as well, so I reckon I shan't have to kill you, I'll have supper in here tonight.' So they brought supper, and another stool for him, and down the two sat.

Well, he hadn't eaten but a mouthful or so when he stops and begins to laugh.

'What is it?' says she.

'Why,' says he, 'I was out hunting today, and I got away to a place in the wood I'd never seen before. And there was an old chalk pit. And I heard a kind of a sort of humming. So I got off my horse and I went right quietly to the pit, and I looked down. Well, what should there be but the funniest little black thing you ever set eyes on. And what was it doing but it had a little spinning wheel and it was spinning wonderfully fast, and twirling its tail. And as it span it sang:

Nimmy nimmy not
My name's Tom Tit Tot.

Well, when the girl heard this she felt as if she could have jumped out of her skin for joy, but she didn't say a word.

Next day the little thing looked so full of malice when he came for the flax. And when night came she heard it knocking against the window panes. She opened the window, and it come right in on the ledge. It was grinning from ear to ear and, ooh, its tail was twirling round so fast.

'What's my name?' it says, as it gave her the skeins.

'Is it Solomon?' she says, pretending to be afraid.

'Nooo, 't'ain't,' it says, and it came further into the room.

'Well, is it Zebedee?' says she again.

'Nooo, 'tain't,' says the imp. And then it laughed and twirled its tail till you could hardly see it.

'Take your time, woman,' it says. 'Next guess, and you're mine.' And it stretched out its black hands at her.

Well, she backed a step or two, and she looked at it, and then she laughed out loud and says, pointing her finger at it:

Nimmy nimmy not
Your name's Tom Tit Tot.

Well, when it heard that it gave an awful shriek and flew away into the dark, and she never saw it any more.

An English Rumpelstiltskin. Joseph Jacobs described this as 'one of the best folk tales that have ever been collected, far superior to any of the continental versions'. It came from a teller in Suffolk and Jacobs said he had 'reduced' the Suffolk dialect. All I have done is slightly update the language just a little more.

TIIDU THE PIPER

This is one of the few tales in this collection that is not from the British Isles. I came across it by accident and it fits so perfectly that I had to include it. Try to guess where it does come from and then read the notes to see if you were right.

Once upon a time there was a poor man who had a wife and ten children – more children than he had bread to feed them! But as soon as they were old enough the children all helped out and worked hard and so they got by. All the children bar one, that is, and that was Tiidu. He was a big, lazy boy. In the summer he liked nothing better than lying under a tree and dreaming and, in winter, rather like Assipattle in the famous Orkney tale of that name, Tiidu liked to laze in the ashes by the fire doing nothing. If there was anything Tiidu did enjoy doing it was playing his whistle and he was quite good at that.

One day he was sitting in a field playing his whistle so sweetly that you could have thought it was a bird singing when an old man came by and congratulated him on his playing and asked him that old question that adults always ask children: 'And what work do you want to do when you grow up?'

Tiidu replied, 'I don't want to work, I want to be rich and have servants to do the work for me.'

'How will you get rich if you don't work?' the man said in a rather annoying way. 'Sleeping cats catch no mice! If you want to get rich you have to work either with your hands or your head.'

'Be quiet, old man,' shouted Tiidu. 'I've told you I don't want to work. No one will ever make a worker out of me.'

The man ignored his rudeness. 'You have a great gift. If you go out into the town and play your whistle you will easily earn enough money to support yourself and if you just spend the minimum you need to feed yourself you will soon be able to save up enough to buy yourself a set of good pipes. Then people will really like what you play and you will earn a lot of money. Try it for a few weeks and see. Then I will come back and see how you are getting on.'

With that the old man went on his way and Tiidu went home and that night he thought about what the old man had said.

Next morning early, Tiidu packed up his whistle and a few clothes and left home. 'He'll soon come home with his tail between his legs when he gets hungry,' said his father. But he didn't. Tiidu went from village to village and played his whistle and people enjoyed it and gave him food and sometimes a bed, and at the end of every day he had a nice little heap of coins – only very small coins, but they added up and soon he had saved enough money to buy himself a cheap set of pipes.

From then on the only way was up. Tiidu found himself in demand to play at parties and dances and christenings and weddings and in no time at all he was able to buy a better set of pipes. With really fine pipes, Tiidu's playing got better and better until there was no finer piper around. His playing was guaranteed to set people dancing and they came from far and near to hear him. This fame stirred him on to even greater things. When he wasn't performing he was practising and when he wasn't practising he was learning and composing new tunes. After a year or two he was such a hard-working musician that his parents would not have recognised him as the lazy boy who would do nothing.

But then something happened.

Fame and fortune can be a burden as well as a blessing. Tiidu forgot the joy he had found in his music and just thought about the money it earned him. He wanted more and more money, although he already had more than he had ever dreamed of. He began to think of other places he could go and other things he could do to make money. His music suffered and at last he stopped playing entirely and tried other jobs, but he was no good at them. He lost everything he had and after a few years he found himself as penniless as he had been when the old man first met him.

With no job and nothing to do, he went and sat in a park and watched all the people walking by in their finery. After a while he saw an old man who looked vaguely familiar. 'Where are your pipes?' he asked, and then Tiidu recognised him. He sat down and Tiidu told him everything that had happened since they last met. 'A fool you were and a fool you will always be,' said the man and told Tiidu to go and fetch his pipes and start playing them there and then, in the park.

Tiidu hadn't played for a long while and at first he was hesitant and rusty but as he played the joy came back to him. A crowd gathered and when he paused he took off his hat, placed it on the ground and people threw coins in it. They begged him to come back and play again next Sunday and soon he was in demand again. In fact, after a few months he had more offers of work than he could manage. He became rich and able to buy anything he wanted – clothes, houses, carriages …

Now Tiidu decided it was time to go home and to show his family that he was a success.

He was greeted by his father and some of his brothers and sisters but he was sorry to find that his mother and others of his siblings had died while he was away. He was made welcome and was able to make the lives of his family comfortable. Then he looked around for a wife and when he found someone they had a grand wedding with tables laden with food, plenty to drink, games and dances and good company.

But those who were there always said that the best part of the day was the hour when they all sat and listened to Tiidu playing his pipes.

Adapted from an Estonian Fairy Tale in Andrew Lang's Crimson Fairy Book, *1903.*

THE PIED PIPER OF FRANCHVILLE

How can you have a book of stories about music and musicians without including the Pied Piper. This, though, is not the universally known story about the German town of Hamelin that the Brothers Grimm and the poet Browning wrote about so famously, this is the Pied Piper of Newtown on the Isle of Wight, or Franchville as it was known in those days.

Today Newtown is a tiny hamlet, just a cluster of houses, on the north-west coast of the island. It is an important archaeological site, being a well-preserved medieval settlement. Newtown was originally called Franchville, or Freetown, and by the fourteenth century it was the most important port on the island. Then something happened and it gradually fell into neglect until it became almost abandoned.

Historians will probably tell you that the change in fortune of Franchville was due to a combination of the plague and the harbour silting up. Because of the plague, there were no young people about to maintain the harbour or to protect it when it was later attacked by the French. But was it the plague that removed all the young people? Or was it the Pied Piper?

Franchville was having trouble with rats. They were everywhere. There had always been some rats – there are in every seaport town – but recently their numbers had been increasing. Now they were out of control. You couldn't walk down the stairs without a rat tripping you up. Mothers couldn't go to bed at night but had to stay by their baby's cradles in case rats came and nibbled them. They didn't just nibble at the food in the larder, they ate every scrap of it and it was not unusual for a housewife to stock up one day and then find an empty pantry the next.

When the trouble started, all the households in Franchville invested in cats. That worked for a while, but gradually the cats were outnumbered until even the most battle-hardened old fighters gave up and sneaked away.

They tried poison but if you're not very careful you finish up by poisoning yourself as well and after that had happened a few times they dropped that idea. It was too dangerous.

And how about rat-catchers? Well, every rat-catcher from Land's End to John o' Groats came to Franchville at one time or another. They came with their traps and their poisons and their fierce little dogs and all kinds of fancy and magical ways of ridding the town of rats. But they all left after a while knowing that this problem was beyond them.

The town council did not know what to do. They'd tried everything.

And then, one day, the Pied Piper arrived.

I don't know where he came from, and no one else did either. He just appeared in the town, walking out of the sea haze like the unknown rider in a spaghetti western. He pushed his way into the town hall and said softly, 'I hear you have a problem.' And he offered to solve the problem in return for the sum of £50, which was a huge amount of money in those days. And the council agreed to pay it because they were so desperate, and they didn't think he could do it anyway.

The Pied Piper was a sight to behold – a very tall, very thin man with a bag on his back. And his clothing wasn't just pied (two-coloured), it contained just about every colour that had ever been dyed into material!

As soon as the bargain was struck, the Pied Piper walked into the street, put his whistle to his lips and started to play a tune – a piercing, shrill, leaping tune, and from every nook and cranny of the town came a flood of leaping, shrieking rats. A tide of rats. There were so many of them that the streets turned black with a liquid wave of writhing bodies. The Piper led the tumbling wave of rats up Silver Street, into Gold Street and on towards the harbour. There he climbed into a boat and, still playing, sailed into the deep water in the middle of the harbour, where he stopped. The rats followed him into the sea and out to where he moored and there they swam round and round the boat as the tide gradually went out. As the water disappeared the rats slowly sunk into the ooze, where they were stuck and when the tide came back in they were all drowned.

Then the Piper sailed to shore, where he was greeted by the cheers of the townsfolk, who clapped and danced and set the church bells ringing.

The only people who weren't delighted were the town council for they did not have £50 in the town's coffers. As every politician that has ever lived will do, they tried to get out of the deal; they tried to bargain and beat the Piper down. They said that anyone could have done what he had done, so why should they pay him £50 for it …

The Piper would have none of it. He insisted that he had a contract for £50, so it was £50 that they must pay. And he warned the council, 'That is not the only tune I can play … you would not want me to play the one I have in mind!'

'What? You have the impudence to threaten us, you strolling vagabond?' the Mayor cried. 'Do your worst. The rats have gone so we don't need you anymore. Be off. Get out of the town before we throw you into the harbour too.'

The Piper put his pipe to his mouth and played a new tune, a rollicking, playful, fun tune, and every child in the town ran and skipped and danced out into the street to join the Piper, who led them from the harbour up Gold Street into Silver Street and out of the town into the forest. The tune and the sound of laughter and dancing feet gradually faded as they ran through the trees from glade to glade and, eventually, it was all swallowed up amidst the old oaks and beeches and the tangled briars and nettles.

It was in vain that the townsfolk of Franchville waited for their children to return. Neither they nor the Piper were ever seen again. It soon became a town populated only by old people, and an air of melancholy that could not be dispelled hung over it. And so, when the French attacked the Isle of Wight a few years later they chose to land at Franchville and there was no one there to protect it.

Slightly adapted from the version in my book Where Dragons Soar and other Animal Folk Tales of the British Isles, *THP, 2016.*

I don't know whether Hamelin or Franchville is the official 'owner' of this really good story. Obviously, Hamelin did a better job of marketing it! Interestingly, there are links between the Grimm / Browning / Hamelin version of the tale and the last story in this book – 'The Devil's Violin from Transylvania'. In Transylvania there are various communities who live fairly peacefully together: Romanians, Hungarians, Gypsies … and before the Second World War there were Jews too. Ever since the twelfth century there has also been a population of 'Saxons', although it has dwindled since the war as many have returned to Germany. Legend has it that they are the descendants of the children the Pied Piper of Hamelin led under the mountains and into the 'land beyond the forest', which is what Transylvania means although, in reality, they were settled there deliberately in much the same way as Protestant gentry were 'planted' in Ireland.

THE MAN WHO STOLE THE PARSON'S SHEEP

In a little village up in the remotest part of the Derbyshire Peak District (for those of you who know the area, I always picture Youlgrave, or somewhere like that) lived a poor man with a large family. He scraped a living as a lead miner and by doing odd jobs all through the year, and they just about got by. But every year, at Christmas, he made sure his family had a really good dinner by stealing a sheep! Everyone knew this happened but they could never prove it because the evidence had always disappeared – been eaten – before they could find it.

One year the sheep he stole happened to belong to the parson.

One morning soon afterwards, this parson was walking down a track near the village when he heard singing. He looked over the dry stone wall and there, playing in the dirt behind the wall, was one of the children from this family – a young lad of 8 or 9 years old.

The parson listened quietly for a few minutes and what the boy was singing was this:

My father's stolen the parson's sheep
So a right good Christmas we shall keep.
We shall have both pudding and meat
And he can't do nothing about it.

'I say, lad,' said the parson. 'You've got a beautiful voice.
You shouldn't keep it a secret, you should let everyone
hear. I'll tell you what. Come along to church on
Sunday and sing to all the congregation. Then they'll
know how well you can sing.'

'Oh, I couldn't do that,' replied the boy. 'I
don't know any songs.'

'Well, that little song you were singing then,
that will do fine,' said the parson.

'No,' said the boy 'I can't come to church
looking like this. My clothes are all ragged
and I haven't got any boots to wear.'

'Don't worry about that,' said the
parson. 'You just come along. I'll
sort you out some clothes and some
new boots.'

And that's what happened. The boy
arrived at the church early on the next
Sunday morning and, before the service,
the parson took him into the vestry and
rigged him out in some second-hand
clothes and some boots that nearly fitted
and then at the end of the service, before
the congregation left, the parson went up
into the pulpit and said, 'Brethren, brethren, before you leave there is something I'd
like you to hear. Living in this village is a
boy who has a beautiful voice and today
he is going to sing for you.'

He beckoned to the boy, who rose from his seat at the back of the church and walked down the aisle. When he reached the front, he turned and faced the congregation – everyone from the village all assembled together. He looked up at the parson and smiled an angelic smile. And then he began to sing:

When I was in the field one day
I saw the parson kiss a maid,
He gave me a shilling not to tell
And these new clothes do suit me well.

This traditional tale is well known in Derbyshire. I included it in my Derbyshire Folk Tales *book (2010). I use it regularly in live performance and it always goes down well. It is from Addy's* Household Tales & Traditional Remains, Collected in the Counties of York, Lincoln, Derby & Nottingham, *David Nutt, 1895.*

TAPPING AT THE BLIND

There was a man, a military man, a colonel in fact, who left it quite late in life to get married but then he married a beautiful young woman and they were blissfully happy. Nine months later, they had a beautiful baby boy and they were even happier.

And then the army spoiled it by, literally, giving him his marching orders – they posted him overseas to fight in a war.

Now this young woman was absolutely distraught about this.

When we have some big problem or something terrible happens we very often don't worry about the big problem, it is too big and frightening to get our thoughts round. Instead we find some silly little insignificant thing and all our worries focus in on that.

So it wasn't the idea of her husband fighting in a war and perhaps being killed or maimed that worried her … it was having to sleep alone!

She'd never slept alone in her life. Before she married the colonel she'd been one of a big family in a small house, so she'd shared her bed with her sisters – two up one way and two up the other – and the idea of that big, empty bed beside her really worried her … for a few days, until she hit upon the answer and went and chatted up a young lieutenant in another regiment who wasn't going overseas and arranged that when bedtime came he would come and tap on the window and she would let him in to fill up that nasty space in the bed.

Problem solved.

The day came for the colonel to leave – he had his trunk packed and was all ready. He said his goodbyes and off he went. The arrangements were all made with the lieutenant, the evening drew nigh ... and then the colonel arrived back home! War had been postponed. But it was too late to postpone the lieutenant, so she had to hope that if she ignored him when he came tapping on the window he'd get fed up and go away.

The colonel was tired after all the coming and going so he climbed into bed and instantly fell asleep. She lay there wondering what would happen when the lieutenant arrived.

Soon she heard him tapping on the blind: tap tap, tap tap, tap tap.

She ignored him and hoped he would just go away ... but he didn't.

Tap tap, tap tap, tap tap. She was worried that it would wake the colonel.

And then she had an idea. She got out of bed, tiptoed over to the cot, pinched the baby so it started to cry and that gave her the excuse to pick it up and rock it and sing a little lullaby:

> It's no use tapping at the blind,
> It's no use tapping at the blind,
> For the baby's at the breast
> And the colonel's in his nest,
> It's no use tapping at the blind.

But she only sang it quietly because she was afraid of waking the colonel and the lieutenant probably didn't hear because he continued tap tap, tap tap, tap tap on the blind.

So she checked that the colonel wasn't stirring and plucked up her courage and sang it a bit louder:

It's no use tapping at the blind,
It's no use tapping at the blind,
For the baby's at the breast
And the colonel's in his nest,
It's no use tapping at the blind.

But still he went on, tap tap, tap tap, tap tap on the blind.

She was just wondering whether she dared sing it again louder still when the colonel solved the problem for her. He sat up in bed and sang out at the top of his voice:

It's no use tapping at the blind,
It's no use tapping at the blind,
For when the baby's finished sucking,
I'm ready for the … loving
It's no use tapping at the blind.

Another story I do a lot, particularly in folk clubs. It came from an EFDSS cassette album of songs collected in Northern Ireland, probably thirty years ago. I used it as the title track of my 2003 album of stories, Tapping at the Blind.

FILL THE HOUSE

A death in a family can give rise to all kinds of contrasting emotions: sometimes it's relief if the person has been suffering for a long while; it can be shock or horror if it happens suddenly and unexpectedly; there can be the sadness that you didn't get to say your goodbyes or to tell them something you should have ... And then there is the will. Many family quarrels and feuds start due to wills; someone doesn't get what they think they deserve or were expecting, someone else gets too much or too little, someone is forgotten, money goes to a charity or a helper rather than a family member ... you know the kind of thing. That is the starting point for this story.

There was a man who was not poor but neither was he rich, and all his money, you could hardly call it a fortune, was tied up in his house; that was the only thing of any consequence that he had to leave after his death.

He had three sons and he pondered long on which one he should leave the house to – he definitely didn't want it to be sold and the money shared out. At last he came up with a plan and had his lawyer write it out very carefully so that there could be no misunderstandings. Then he could relax.

After a while the man died and was buried and his sons mourned him as they should. Then came the day for the will to be read and they all went to the lawyer's office to hear what their father had decided.

It is very difficult to describe exactly what he said because I can't speak in lawyer's language, and if I could you probably wouldn't understand it; lawyers seem to make things as incomprehensible as possible! Basically, he had set his sons a competition. Each in turn was to attempt to fill the house with anything they chose and the one who succeeded in doing it best, in the eyes of the lawyer, would inherit. They were given a few weeks to prepare.

In true folk tale fashion, the eldest son went first. He had spent his preparation time in buying every oil lamp, candle, rush light and torch he could lay his hands on. He set them out all round the house and just before the lawyer was due for the inspection he ran round the house from top to bottom lighting them all.

The lawyer entered the front door and was greeted by a house full of light. He went through all the ground floor rooms and up the stairs

– all ablaze with light. The bedrooms were brightly lit too. Then up the smaller stairs – not quite so brightly lit – to the attics where the lights were beginning to gutter and go out. Some of the recesses just had a haze of smoke showing where there had been light. But he had done quite well.

A few days later it was the turn of the middle son. He had begged, borrowed or bought every eiderdown, pillow, quilt, duvet he could find and as the lawyer arrived he went round the house ripping them open and scattering feathers everywhere. It worked well and the first rooms were a snowstorm of feathers (it's a good job the lawyer did not suffer from asthma!) but by the time he'd finished in the attic bedrooms they were sinking to the floor. Again he had done well and it was very difficult to tell who would be the winner.

So we come to the youngest son. No one had seen any signs of him doing any preparation – no deliveries, nothing being bought …

When the lawyer arrived there was no sign of anything different, just the front door slightly ajar. He went in. Nothing. No lights, no feathers, nothing that he could see … He went from room to room. No youngest son either. The lawyer began to get cross. 'He's let his father down,' he thought. 'He hasn't even attempted the task.' He went round the house to try to find him and as he did so he realised that he must be there because he could hear him. The youngest son was a very accomplished whistle player and he was somewhere in the house playing his whistle.

'Lazy young good-for-nothing,' he thought.

But his music was very nice and the lawyer began to smile. As he went up the stairs he even found himself giving a little skip. He went through every room in the house and wherever he went there was the music. Eventually he found the young man in the furthest reaches of the furthest attic leaning on a beam and playing a jolly tune. The lawyer could not prevent himself from tapping his foot and joining in. When the boy eventually stopped playing, the lawyer had a big smile on his face.

'I'm very disappointed in you,' he said, trying to look serious. 'Your brothers attempted to do the task your father set but you haven't done anything at all.'

'I beg to differ,' replied the boy. 'I would argue that I have filled the house far more successfully than either of my brothers. In fact I have filled the house three times over!'

'How so?' Asked the lawyer.

'I think you would agree that wherever you went in the house you could hear my whistle, so I have filled the house with music. And I know that you tapped your feet and you did a little skip a few times, so I have filled the house with dancing. And, although you pretend you are angry with me, I saw you smile and heard you joining in my song, so I have also filled the house with happiness.'

'Music, dancing, happiness,' mused the lawyer. 'Yes, I have to agree.'

And so the youngest son inherited the house. The older ones murmured and moaned, as did others in the family and some local people. 'What did he do to deserve it?' they asked. 'He just played his whistle. Anyone could have done that. And he didn't do any preparation – just played for the short time the lawyer was in the house ...'

But is that true? Did he inherit the house just because he played his whistle for, say, half an hour?

No, he inherited the house because he had spent days and weeks and months and years learning to play the whistle and yet more time honing his skill until he became a really good player.

The same is true when you hear people complaining about a musician wanting a huge fee for just a few minutes' work. You are not paying him just for the hour he's on stage, you are paying for all the rehearsal and practice and learning, the thought about what to play when and the skill learned from many, many other performances that enables him (or her, of course) to deliver what you want when you want it. Glasgerion would understand.

Many years ago I heard Taffy Thomas tell this story and asked him if he minded if I told it, too. He didn't. As it turned out, I didn't use it very often because I wasn't satisfied with the ending – which I have now changed. When I came to write this book I tried to find out more about the story but could find nothing so I went back to the source and asked Taffy, who said:

I can tell you about collecting the story, it came to me orally. I was telling stories at Saffron Walden Festival, it could have been late eighties or early nineties, and one evening after my show I was chatting and telling stories over a cup of cocoa with the wardens at the Hostel. One of them asked me if I knew this story he had known as a child and gave it to me to tell. It became one of the favourite stories of my repertoire. He told it as a farmer's tale and I haven't found any other origin. It's always one of the favourite stories I tell if I have a musician with me.

I hope all this helps, as you say it would go well in a book about the link between music and story, and it would be great to credit how the stories have links to being collected by storytellers like me in the oral tradition.

His version can be found in two of Taffy's History Press publications: in The Riddle in the Tale *as 'Filling the House' and in* Lakeland Folk Tales for Children *as 'The Farmer's Fun-loving Daughter'. I've made a point of not looking at either so I don't know how far mine has diverged from the 'original'.*

THE SHOW MUST
GO ON

This story follows on from the previous one very nicely because it came to me in much the same way that 'Fill the House' was given to Taffy.

I did a Halloween performance for a group of young people – mainly late teens or early 20s. I can't remember what the group was exactly but I think it was a charity to help young people with mental health problems or addictions or something like that. Anyway, it went well and they were very enthusiastic. When I'd finished, they brought out refreshments – tea, coffee, soft drinks and cakes decorated with Halloween motifs … that sort of thing. While we were eating, I noticed a little group with their heads together discussing or planning something. After a while they came up and said, 'Can we tell you a story we've just made up?' This is it.

It had become a tradition that every year on the Saturday nearest to Halloween the Storyteller would come and present his show of spooky stories. It had happened for several years and didn't need much organising: The Organiser got the room ready, the Storyteller arrived and did his thing; the Audience came and listened and had a good time. That was it. This year the Organiser realised that he hadn't heard from the Storyteller but it was too late to do anything about it now – the show was tonight.

He needn't have worried. The Organiser opened the hall, the Audience rolled up ... But where was the Storyteller? Just as the Organiser was beginning to get concerned, he arrived, in the nick of time, looking a bit hassled but ready to go. The evening was as good as it always was. Everyone enjoyed it, there were several encores and, at the end, the Organiser paid the Storyteller his money, said, 'Goodbye, see you next time,' and that was it for another year ...

When the Organiser arrived home he picked up the post. There were some circulars and a couple of bills and one proper letter that read:

Dear Sir
This is to let you know that the Storyteller won't be able to do his show of ghost stories this year. He died last week.

But the show must go on and we Storytellers are as good dead as alive!

THE GROVE OF HEAVEN

Not all music is made by people. Nature is full of music. We can hear it in the sighing of the wind, the rustling of leaves and the pounding of the waves. Many people have been inspired or comforted by the music performed by birds – Vaughan Williams' famous piece 'The Lark Ascending' springs to mind. I have found that if you sit and play music quietly in a secluded spot – a garden, a churchyard or a woodland glade – birds will often come and join in. It is a magical experience. There is a famous recording, which you can find online, of one of the BBC's first ever outside broadcasts, made in May 1914 of the cellist Beatrice Harrison playing in her garden and being accompanied by a nightingale.

Here is a story with a similar theme:

There was once a pious monk, we'll call him Brother Godfrey, whose only delight in life was in prayer and meditation and in living the holiest life possible.

One evening Godfrey was wandering through the wood near the monastery, following the stream as it tumbled over rocks. He was deep in thought and oblivious to everything until a bird burst into song nearby. Godfrey was entranced and stopped to listen. It was, he thought, the most beautiful music he had ever heard, more beautiful even than the monks themselves singing at their best, and surely the bird must be praising god.

Godfrey stood listening, not daring to move in case he scared the bird away. He stood there, almost in a dream, for a long while and when the bird had finished its song he turned and made his way back to the monastery. He felt uplifted and full of the glory of creation.

When he got there the monastery building was unchanged but the gardens looked different, and when he went in he didn't recognise any of the monks – and they didn't recognise him. They gathered round and asked him who he was and he tried to explain that he was one of them and he'd been out for a walk and had just stopped to listen to a bird singing and now everything had changed.

Godfrey asked to be put in a cell so that he could pray.

In the morning the cell was empty apart from a handful of ashes on the floor.

The monks did some research and discovered that several hundred years before a monk had left the monastery for a walk and had never returned and no trace of him was ever found.

They decided that Brother Godfrey was that monk and the wood where he listened to the bird's song they called the Grove of Heaven.

A Welsh tale.

THE FIDDLER AND
THE BEARDED LADY

In the little church of St Mary in the Norfolk village of Worstead is an ancient icon showing a bearded lady hanging on a cross. She is wearing a crown, a long dress and has gold boots on her feet. To one side, at the foot of the cross, is a tiny fiddler playing his fiddle. It's a strange combination of images and it tells a strange story.

The woman is St Wilgefortis, who is often known in England as Uncumber. Often known …? Well, she's not very well known in Britain these days but she was known throughout Europe in the Middle Ages under various names and was a special saint for women, who would pray to her for help against oppressive or cruel husbands.

Wilgefortis was a devout young Christian woman who had decided to live a life of celibacy but her father, an important man and a pagan, arranged for her to marry. He would not listen to her pleas and the wedding was set to go ahead, so Wilgefortis prayed that God would make her so ugly that no one would want to marry her! When she woke the next morning she had grown a full beard of which any man would have been proud. Not surprisingly, the marriage was called off.

When she tried to reason with her father and explain how and why she had done what she had done, her father ordered her to be cruci-fied – 'like the god she was so fond of!'

Hence the main part of the image.

Wilgefortis was made a saint and statues and icons of her appeared all over Europe.

Why she was depicted wearing golden boots I don't know, but one day a destitute fiddler came upon her statue and he saw women making offerings to her. He was poor and had nothing to offer but his music, so he played a tune before the statue, which kicked off one of its golden boots towards him.

He took it to a smith to have it melted down but the smith assumed he had stolen it and reported him and the fiddler was arrested. He pleaded his innocence and tried to explain what had happened but no one believed him. Eventually he was allowed to go and play another tune in front of the statue in front of wit-nesses and, low and behold, it kicked off its other boot towards him and so proved his innocence!

That is why he appears in the icon.

That is the story. How and why it grew up is another story in its own right. Very often with stories that set out to explain physical things, we don't know whether it was a pre-existing story that was attached to an object or whether the object inspired someone to make up a story to explain how it came to be. (A third option is that it might be true, of course!)

The explanation for this image, and hence the story, is very simple. When we see images of the crucifixion, whether they are Renaissance paintings or modern crucifixes, we are used to seeing Christ hanging on the cross wearing a crown of thorns and a loincloth. That has been the tradition for centuries. But it wasn't always so. Before the iconography became set he might have been portrayed wearing different clothes – perhaps even a long robe.

So, once upon a time, there was an image of Christ on the cross with a crown of thorns, a full beard and a long robe. Someone saw it and mistook it for a bearded lady and the story of St Wilgefortis emerged …

The cult of Wilgefortis was widespread but had fallen out of favour in Northern Europe by the sixteenth century. There is a fine carving of Wilgefortis, in which she is definitely a woman, in the Henry VII chapel at Westminster Abbey in London. The illustration is based on a statue in a museum in Gras, Austria. The story of the fiddler was probably created and added to the legend in the thirteenth century.

JOSEPH AND THE BULL

Young Joseph – he was called 'Young' Joseph to distinguish him from his father 'Old' Joseph, who must also have been Young Joseph at one time because his father had been Joseph, too – lived in a little agricultural village not far from Dorchester in Dorset. He earned his very meagre living by doing odd jobs and seasonal work on several of the local farms but he added a tiny amount to it through his violin playing. He wasn't a brilliant violinist but he was adequate and could do what was needed.

This was in the days before the established church carried out a big modernisation and did away with the West Galleries and the singers and musicians who performed in them and replaced the church bands with new-fangled harmoniums and organs and the old hymns and carols with new ones that the people did not like half as much.

Young Joseph played in the church band alongside several other musicians on viol, clarinet, flute and serpent. The same group, augmented by a drum and cymbal, played for village dances, so they were kept quite busy. (Drums were frowned on in the church and no one would dare take one in, let alone play it.)

Young Joseph, who at the time of this story wasn't that young – he was nearing 50, had learned to keep the two aspects of his music making separate ever since the occasion, a few years ago, when they had played at a village dance on Saturday evening, had a lot too much to drink, and attended the Sunday morning service very much the worse for wear. The musicians had all dozed off during a long, very boring sermon, and when someone suddenly woke them and said, 'Play the next piece,' they had forgotten where they were and played the next dance rather than the next hymn!

So, this Saturday evening Young Joseph was making his way home after playing at a village 'do' and was feeling slightly woozy, but not drunk. He knew he would be alright by morning. Now though, not being fully aware, he made a horrible mistake. Rather than take the long way home round the road, he found himself taking a short-cut across Farmer Jones' Long Meadow. Normally that would have been alright but Joseph had forgotten that Farmer Jones had put his bull into the Long Meadow and it was well known as a particularly unpredictable bull. Joseph remembered this when, through the evening gloom, he saw a large shape rise up from the ground in front of him. The bull was obviously in one of his bad moods when he would not tolerate anyone coming into 'his' field. He turned towards Joseph, lowered his head and roared. Joseph knew full well that a bull can easily outrun the fastest man around and a slightly overweight, unfit, tipsy fiddle player had no chance of beating it to the gate. If he was going to be killed by a bull he thought he might as well go out feeling happy and what made him feel happy was playing his fiddle, so he took it out of its case, tucked it under his chin and began to play his favourite tune, 'The Devil Among the Tailors'.

Farmer Jones' bull turned out to be a music lover. It stopped bellowing and stood still. Joseph played on, played it through several times, and then he stopped. The bull immediately lowered its head and pawed the ground. So Joseph played another tune, another lively dance tune. And so the evening went on. As it grew darker and darker, Joseph played all through his repertoire of dance tunes: 'The Dashing White Sergeant', 'Jockey to the Fair', 'The Tailors Breeches' ... dozens of them. Then he started playing songs, singing along to his fiddle playing 'The Barley Mow', 'The Seeds of Love', 'The Banks of Allen Water' and, of course, 'I've Lost My Spotted Cow' (he thought the bull might like that one!). When he couldn't think of any more songs, he moved on to the hymns and psalms they used in church: 'Abide With Me', 'Are You Washed in the Blood', 'When the Roll is Called Up Yonder', 'While Shepherds Watched', and anything else he could think of. All the while he played, the bull was calm and quiet, at one point it even laid down, but as soon as Joseph paused the bull was up on its feet and threatening to charge.

The moon rode across the sky, the sky went from grey to pitch black and back to grey again. A touch of yellow and pink rose from the eastern horizon. By now Joseph had played every tune he knew, and some he didn't, several times over and he was so tired that he could hardly raise his bow. He felt his knees begin to give way and thought he would fall asleep there and then. But then another tune flashed into his mind, one he hadn't played so far. It was a carol used on Christmas Eve. He started to play it. It would be a good tune to end his life on, he thought. He was expecting the bull to charge at any second, but it didn't, instead it bent its knees and put its head on the ground and closed its eyes. Then Joseph remembered an old superstition. People believed that at midnight on Christmas Eve the farm animals went down on their knees and worshipped god in memory of Jesus being born in a stable. The bull had obviously recognised the carol as the one played on Christmas Eve and acted accordingly.

Joseph did not waste time thinking about it though, he left his fiddle case lying where it was and ran as fast as his legs would carry him for the gate while the bull was still lost in its prayers.

And that is the story of Young Joseph and the Bull.

Several stories combined. Playing the Christmas carol for the bull is a traditional tale that Thomas Hardy (one of my favourite authors) borrowed and used in Tess of the D'Urbervilles. *Tim Laycock included it in* Dorset Folk Tales. *The band who play a dance tune instead of the next hymn is also borrowed from Hardy – a short story called 'Absent-Mindedness in a Choir'. That big reorganisation also led to the 'pub carol' tradition of North Derbyshire/South Yorkshire, where the old carols that are no longer sung in church are sung in pubs in the Christmas period.*

I regularly go walking in the Derbyshire countryside and we often go through fields of cows, often with a bull. I always have in the back of my mind the fact that only an Olympic 100m runner can outpace a bull – or a cow – if it really wants to get you!

BRAGI

It seems to have been a prerequisite for ancient leaders to also be musicians. King David, the psalmist in the Bible, springs to mind, as do many gods, kings, lords etc. in Greek, Irish and Welsh mythology … but not English for some reason. We know that Henry VIII loved music and Richard I is mentioned as a songwriter earlier in this book, but no English king seems to have had a magic harp!

Bragi was a lesser-known Nordic god, the god of poetry, eloquence and song, and Viking bards or storytellers were sometimes called Braga-men. We might get our word for boasting from Bragi. When a leader died and a new one took his place, the menfolk drank his health and swore to do a great deed to prove their loyalty. This had to be accomplished within a year. (Perhaps that's where the ubiquitous year-and-a-day of folk tales comes from?) Sometimes, particularly if they had already had slightly too much drink, they would promise to do things that were impossible to achieve – hence bragging.

Bragi is a vague figure believed to be a son of Odin and his wife Gunlod. He was born in a stalactite-hung cave deep in the earth and the dwarfs presented him with a golden harp, placed him in a boat and set him adrift on a subterranean river. The boat sailed down the river until it passed by the realm of Nain, the dwarf of death. Then Bragi, who had shown no signs of life to that point, suddenly sat up, picked up the harp and sang the Song of Life, which soared up to heaven and reached down to hell.

While he played, the boat emerged into the sunlight and drifted gently across the waters of a lake until it touched on the far shore. Bragi climbed out of the boat and walked over the barren land and through the bare forests, and as he did so he played his harp and flowers sprang up from the earth and the trees burst into leaf. Then he met a young woman of unbelievable beauty. She was Iduna, the goddess of youth, who the dwarfs allowed out of the underworld occasionally. As soon as they met they fell in love – such a pair must have been destined for each other – and Bragi took her as his wife. Together they journeyed to Asgard, where the gods greeted them and Odin was impressed by Bragi's songs and Iduna's beauty.

Iduna, as goddess of eternal youth, kept with her a box of apples and when the gods began to grow old all they needed to do was take a bite of an apple to regain their strength and vitality.

'An apple a day …'

Bragi then disappears from the story, so we must assume that he remained in Asgard as Odin's skald, singing praises to every visitor who came and went and reciting the histories of the gods and their adventures. Eventually he presided over Valhalla, where those who died well in battle went and were joined by the best musicians and poets. A fitting end.

From Norse mythology. It seems as though there must be more to the story of Bragi but despite searching and consulting experts I have been unable to find it.

KING ORFEO

Der lived a king into da aist
Skoven arle grön
Der lived a lady in da wast
Hvor hjorten han gar arlig

Dis king he has a huntin geen
An left his lady Isabel alane.

Oh, I wiss ye'd never geen away
For at your hame it's dule an wae.

For the King o Faerie wi his dairt
His pierced your lady ti da hert.

An eftir them the king is geen
But when he cam it wis a grey stane

Dan he took oot his pipes to play
But sair his hert wi dule an wac.

An first he played da notes o noy,
An dan he played da notes o joy.

Noo he's geen in inta dir haa,
An he's geen in among them aa.

Dan he took oot his pipes to play
But sair his hert wi dule an wae.

Noo tell tac us what you will hae,
What sall we gie you for you play?

What I will hae I will you tell
An dat's me Lady Isabel.

Yees tak yir lady an yees gane harne
An yees be king o'er aa yir ain.

This is a very early British/Scandinavian version of the tale of Orpheus and Euridice where the Greek Underworld has been replaced by Elfland. Professor Francis James Child included a set of words from a printed source of 1880, but surmised that no tune still existed. Then, in 1952, John Stickle of Unst, the northernmost of the Shetland Isles, sang folklorist and collector Patrick Shuldham-Shaw what he described as 'a piece of nonsense' – he had no idea what it meant – but Shaw recognised it. The two refrain lines are almost Scandinavian for 'The wood early turns green' and 'Where the hart goes yearly'.

Child #19. British/Scandinavian. The American scholar Bertrand Bronson, who traced the tunes to most of the Child Ballads, wrote: 'That a tune should in the midst of the twentieth century be recovered for this whisper from the Middle Ages was as little to be expected as that we should hear a horn from elfin-land blowing.' Several people have recorded it but, to my mind, the best version is by Scottish singer Archie Fisher on his 1970 Decca LP Orfeo.

DAGDA'S HARP

There are old stories and there are very old stories ... while some stories that seem old aren't. Some that don't seem old turn out to have very old roots. You just don't know with stories!

This *is* a very old story taken from Irish mythology. It could be the oldest story in this collection – at least the events it tells of happened a very long time ago.

At the end of the last Ice Age – 10,000 years ago – the islands of Britain were empty of people. There had been visiting groups of hunter-gatherers in the slightly warmer periods but no resident population. As the ice retreated and the climate grew milder – which happened amazingly quickly – tribes moved north from the havens in Spain and the Balkans where they had spent the last few thousand years. They were following the sun and the herds and searching for new opportunities. One of the main routes was up the west coast of Europe and across the area of low, marshy land, which was to become the English Channel, into the west of England, Wales and Ireland. Other groups took the slower route up the Danube into northern Europe and Scandinavia and then across Dogger Land – later the North Sea.

These groups were probably very small and they came one after the other over thousands of years. A new group would probably come into conflict with the previous ones who were jealous of 'their' land and so a series of conflicts were fought between them. We have no idea what these people called themselves. They probably all just thought of themselves as people and those who were not in their tribe were probably not proper 'people'. Three of these groups have been recorded in the ancient Irish mythologies as the Firbolgs, the Formorians and the Tuatha Dé Danaan.

They say that the Tuatha Dé Danaan landed in the north of Ireland about 4,000 years ago in a storm of thick clouds that blotted out the sun for three days. They drove out the Firbolgs, who were already living there, and went to war against the Formorians.

Dagda was the leader of the Tuatha Dé Danaan, whose main base was at Brú na Bóinne, the ancient site we now call New Grange. He was a huge, bearded man who wore a cloak. He was both a king and a druid.

When the Tuatha Dé Danaan came to Ireland, Dagda brought with him three priceless treasures: a club that he could use one end of to kill and the other to heal; a cauldron that never ran empty and which could feed as many people as necessary; and his harp called Uaithne or

Four Angled Music. This harp could play magical melodies that stirred his men into deeds of great bravery and bloodlust when going into battle, but calmed and consoled them afterwards when they rested and thought of their fallen comrades. It could also make people weep with sorrow or laugh with joy and it made sure that the seasons came in the right order. With this harp Dagda and the Tuatha Dé Danaan were invincible ... so the Formorians decided to steal Dagda's harp!

They waited until Dagda was embroiled in the midst of a battle and then a party stole into his hall and stole the harp. They took it away to the Formorian camp and hung it on the wall in the main hall where it would be surrounded by warriors when they returned from battle.

When the Tuatha Dé Danaan returned to their camp they called on Dagda to play his harp for them but he discovered it was missing. He guessed instantly where it was and he and his son Aengus Óg went to the Formorian camp to retrieve it. They peeped into the hall where it was being kept but it was full of enemy warriors. There was no chance of taking it. But Dagda sung out to the harp:

Come to me apple-sweet murmurer
Come, four-angled frame of harmony,
Come summer, come winter,
Come to my hand, now!

And the harp sprang off the wall and flew to Dagda. The Formorians sprang to their feet and grabbed their weapons.

'Play your harp,' shouted Aengus and Dagda played the 'Song of Mirth'. The Formorians went into helpless paroxysms of laughter and rolled on the floor. They hooted with laughter and danced and capered. But as soon as Dagda stopped playing they picked up their weapons again and advanced on him.

'Play your harp,' shouted Aengus and Dagda played the 'Song of Grief'. The Formorians wept and the tears ran down their faces. They hid their heads and tore their hair but, again, as soon as Dagda stopped playing they picked up their weapons and advanced on him.

'Play your harp,' shouted Aengus and Dagda played the 'Song of Sleep'. It was so quiet that he seemed not to be playing at all but every one of the Formorians fell into a deep sleep. Dagda and Aengus took the harp and went home.

The wars continued and, eventually, the Tuatha Dé Danaan were victorious and ruled successfully in Ireland for many years until they were defeated by another group of immigrants from north-west Iberia, the Milesians. As part of the peace negotiations the two groups decided to share the country; the Milesians lived above the ground and became the Irish, while the Tuatha Dé Danaan went below and eventually became the Sidhe, or fairies. And many people will tell you that they are still there!

From the oldest books of Irish mythology. It leads nicely on to the next one.

ETAIN AND MIDIR

Etain of the Tuatha Dé Dannan was the most beautiful young woman you are ever likely to see. A bard who saw her sang of her skin as white as the snow of a single night, her eyes of hyacinth blue, her lips of Parthian red and her hair of yellow gold, tied into two tresses, each tress a weaving of four twists with a globe at the end.

Midir was similarly one of the most noble among young men – strong and handsome, intelligent and caring. Unfortunately he lost an eye when a boy threw a sprig of holly. This was blamed on Aengus Óg, who was able to find a healer to restore Midir's eye. To make amends, he arranged that Midir should meet Etain, who was considered the most beautiful woman in Ireland. As soon as they met they began a passionate love affair. For a while they were blissfully happy and unaware of anything except each other, but Midir was already married and eventually the time came when he had to return home to his wife, Fuamnach. When you are in love you do not think straight. You imagine that what you would like to happen will happen and Midir thought that he could take Etain home with him and that the two women would like each other and live peaceably together. Of course, he was wrong! Fuamnach was, understandably, deeply hurt and turned her wrath on Etain.

She turned Etain into a shower of rain, which fell into a pool and then condensed into a tiny, jewelled fly. But this did not work to separate Etain and Midir. They would not be parted and she flew around him and sat on his shoulder and whispered into his ear and Midir continued to love Etain just as much.

Fuamnach grew more and more angry and increasingly jealous. She could not bear to hear the buzzing of the fly or catch a glimpse of it as it flew around the room. As tiny as Etain was, she filled a larger and larger space in Fuamnach's mind and her anger grew accordingly. At last she could stand it no longer and Fuamnach conjured up a storm to blow the fly away.

For seven years Etain was blown hither and thither until she chanced to arrive at the castle of Aengus Óg, who knew her immediately for the Tuatha cannot hide themselves from each other. Aengus built her a sunny bower surrounded by scented trees and fountains where she lived happily.

But Fuamnach became aware that Etain was still alive and wanted her even further away, so she conjured up another, even greater, tempest. Etain was sucked up into the clouds, battered by wind and rain, carried through the skies for another seven years until she was blown through a window and into the hall of Etar, a mortal Lord of a territory called Echrad far away in the north of Ulster. Etain landed in a goblet of wine standing on the table in front of the queen just at the very moment she lifted the goblet to drink. Unknowingly, she swallowed Etain.

At that very instant the queen became pregnant and nine months later Etain was reborn as a mortal woman with no knowledge of her previous life. Her beauty and character were the same as ever though, and Etar and his wife raised her as their own daughter and were very proud of her.

When she grew up, Etain married Eochaid Airem, the High King of Ireland, and that came about in the following way:

Eochaid had been High King for several years and ruled Ireland from his dun at Tara but there was murmuring and dissatisfaction amongst his courtiers because he wasn't married. In all other ways he was a good king but it was usual for a king to be married and they felt unable to take their own wives to the court of an unmarried king. So Eochaid sent out his messengers to find him a wife.

They searched throughout Ireland and at last took word back to the king that they had found a suitable bride living with her father in the distant territory of Echrad. When High King Eochaid heard the glowing reports about Etain he set out to find her and woo her.

When he was nearing his journey's end he came upon a spring of clear water hidden in a green glade and there was a woman who could only be Etain surrounded by her maidens preparing to bathe. She wore a tunic of green silk embroidered with gold and tossed on the grass at her side was a rich mantle that she had just taken off. A comb of gold and silver and a jewelled mirror were also ready. Etain and her maidens were talking and laughing and Eochaid had never seen such a beautiful sight.

He rode forward, introduced himself and explained that he had ridden many miles to find her and to ask her to be his bride. Etain immediately accepted him and said that, although many had courted her she had refused them all because she had loved him from afar for many years because of the many stories she had heard about his kindness and goodness as well as his bravery and prowess in battle.

Eochaid paid a great bride price to Etain's father, Etar, and took her back with him to Tara, where they were married in a grand wedding.

Etain immediately won over all Eochaid's courtiers and they all fell in love with her to some degree and felt rewarded if she looked at them, and even more so when she spoke to them. She was equally as kind to the servants and serving maids as she was to the nobles. From then on it was a court full of happiness in all things bar one, and that was Etain's music.

Etain loved music and was a skilled singer and musician but whenever she played the harp and sang all who heard it were filled with a deep sadness and longing that they could not explain. Their hearts ached and tears ran down their cheeks. Her songs seemed to tell of a land and a time more distant than they could imagine and a great loss and pining for something or someone they could not put into words. It almost seemed to be an immortal loss of something from another world.

However sad the music made them it was a satisfying sort of sadness and everyone loved to hear Etain sing. With her at its heart the court thrived and Etain and Eochaid lived happily for many years.

King Eochaid had a brother, Ailill, to whom he was very close. One day when they were all dining together Ailill's wife noticed that her husband seemed quiet and withdrawn. He wasn't joining in with any of the merriment or conversation. He was gazing at something that seemed just out of vision, in a world of his own. Ailill denied that anything was wrong and tried to behave normally but later he had to admit to himself that all was not well. He was in love with Etain, his brother's wife.

Ailill went home and tried to ignore his feelings but instead of time healing, his love sickness became worse and worse and he had to take to his bed, where he stayed for a year unable to do anything but dream of Etain. Eochaid saw how ill his brother was but had no idea of the cause. He sent his best physician to him and he realised that it was no normal sickness but was either an illness brought about by guilt or by love, but Ailill would say nothing about it so the doctor could not help and went away, leaving Ailill to grow weaker and weaker in his bed.

The time came for Eochaid, as the High King of Ireland, to make a great circuit of his realm to visit his people, to listen to their complaints and make judgements and to oversee all the subordinate kings. He was to leave Etain at home and he charged her to look after his brother Ailill while he was gone and gave instructions on how he was to be buried if he died.

Soon after Eochaid had left, Etain visited Ailill to see how he was and to see if there was any way in which she, as a woman and a relative, could help. She found him very weak and unable to leave his bed or to eat. After they had spoken for a while Etain decided that she knew what the ailment was – it wasn't anything physical, it was down to love. She told Ailill what she suspected and said, 'If it is one of my handmaidens who has stolen your heart just tell me and I will court her for you.'

'You are right, my Lady,' said Ailill, 'It is love which is dragging me down. Love and guilt and the impossibility of solving the problem. The only ending will be in my death!'

Etain tried to comfort him and told him that there is always a way to solve a problem but Ailill burst into tears and told her that she was wrong because she was the problem, he was in love with her.

Etain was overcome with sorrow and feelings for the young man. What was she to do? All kinds of ideas flashed through her mind and then she said, 'If I am the cause of your sufferings then I cannot just let you die. There is a way to cure you of this love-sickness.' And she arranged to meet Ailill on the following morning at a place midway between his dun and her home at Tara. Then she left him and Ailill fell into a deep sleep, an unnatural sleep that lasted until long after the time of the agreed tryst.

When Etain arrived at the trysting place she met a young man who looked like Ailill and who was wearing clothes like Ailill's but wasn't quite Ailill. He asked her to make love to him to cure him of his love-sickness but Etain wouldn't. There was something not quite right. Instead she returned home.

The following day Etain visited Ailill, who apologised profusely for missing the meeting they had arranged. He explained that he had fallen into a strange sleep in which his love for her had been washed away. Now he was sensible again and could continue his life and enjoy Etain as his sister-in-law and friend and nothing more. When Eochaid returned from his travels he was overjoyed to find Ailill healed and he congratulated Etain on caring for him so well.

Not long after this Etain was alone in her bower when she was suddenly greeted by a handsome, young warrior. She didn't know him but knew immediately that he was one of the Tuatha Dé Dannan. 'Greetings Etain,' he said. 'I have come to take you home to the Land of Youth where you belong. We have been waiting for you for far too long.' Etain asked who he was and what he meant and he picked up a harp and began to sing.

At this point in the story some tellers and authors have attempted to write the words of the song the young man sang but their efforts are dead and pedestrian. How can you put music on a page? How can you put the many dimensions of fairy music on a page made of earthly wood pulp? He sang of the land of the Tuatha, and the beauty and happiness of its inhabitants, the simple pain-free lives they lived where there was no worry or want. Of how Etain would be greeted and treasured when she returned and of how they would spend the rest of eternity living together in happiness. His notes and words melded together and, at the same time, Etain saw rainbow colours, smelt the most fragrant scents and tasted the most delicious flavours, and it was all in one over-powering sensation that spoke to all her senses at once.

As he sang, all the images that had played through Etain's dreams over many years ran through her head and began to make sense. Half-remembered places and people coalesced, and a life before her parents that she had always thought was imagination, began to take on a reality.

'Who are you?' she asked. 'Why should I betray my husband and go off with a stranger?'

'You were mine before you ever knew your husband and you were willing to betray him with his brother. It was I who stopped you doing that by placing a magic sleep on Ailill. I am Midir of the Tuatha Dé Dannan and we were together long, long ago.'

Midir than explained to Etain how she had been turned into a fly and had spent many years being blown by the winds before dropping into a goblet and being swallowed. Then she was born again and had become Eochaid's wife. As he told the story, Etain realised that it was all true and longed to accompany him but she could not betray her husband Eochaid.

'I will come with you gladly,' she said, 'if Eochaid grants us permis-sion, but I will not sneak away like a thief.' So Etain returned to Tara and soon Eochaid joined her there.

One day he was looking out over the battlements when he became aware of a young man standing beside him. The young man introduced himself as Midir of the Tuatha and said he had heard that Eochaid was a great player of the board game fidchell and he would like to test his skills against him. Eochaid always enjoyed playing the game, so he agreed to play on condition that Midir would carry out a task he set if he lost. He did lose and Eochaid set him to clear all the rocks and stones from the plains of Meath around Tara. With the help of the Dé Dannan, Midir accomplished this in one night.

They played again. Again Midir lost and had to cut down the Forest of Breg.

A third time and his task was to build a causeway across the moor of Lamrach.

Midir was able to do these seemingly impossible tasks.

Then Midir approached Eochaid again wearing his armour and with an angry expression on his face. 'You have used me very harshly for losing a simple game. Let us play once more and if I lose again I will go away for ever, but if I win I will demand one simple thing of you.'

So they played once more and Midir won. 'You have won,' said Eochaid, 'What is it you want?'

'I could have won every time,' said Midir, 'but I chose not to. I want but one simple thing, to hold Etain in my arms and give her one simple kiss.'

'You shall have your wish, but not now. Go away and come back in one month and you shall have what you desire.'

At the end of the month Eochaid had assembled the largest army ever seen in Ireland. They were arrayed rank upon rank all around Tara so that Midir could not gain entry even if he returned at the head of the whole host of the Tuatha Dé Dannan.

But he didn't. He just appeared next to Eochaid and Etain as they stood in their room in the centre of their fortress.

'I have come to take Etain as we agreed,' he said.

'We agreed nothing of the sort. We agreed that you would take her in your arms and give her one kiss and then depart, so that is what you can do.'

Midir put one arm round Etain, kissed her lips, and then together they rose into the sky through a roof window and soared overhead as two white swans that turned southwards and were never seen again …

(Well, they did return but that is a whole different story!)

From 'The Wooing of Etaine' (Tochmarc Étaíne), which comes from the Irish Mythological Cycle that dates back to at least the eighth century CE.

GLASGERION PART 2

Earlier, we left the great bard Glasgerion at the end of an evening of playing and singing in the great hall. The evening was winding down, people were going home or falling asleep where they were. As she left, the Lady – the most beautiful woman in the place, had invited Glasgerion to her room to make love to her. He had been amazed and flattered. He had had his offers before but had usually let them pass. This time, he decided, he would follow it up because, at his age, he might never get the opportunity again!

So Glasgerion said his farewells, wrapped his harp in its green velvet cloth, and hurried back home to where his apprentice, Tom, was waiting.

'You'll never believe what has happened,' he said. 'As she left the hall the Lady whispered that before the night is out I have to visit her in her chamber, to share her bed!'

Glasgerion continued to chatter and laugh about what was going to happen like a teenager on his first date while Tom fetched him a warm drink and made him comfortable in his room.

'Have a sleep,' he said, 'so that you are fit and full of life for the Lady. Don't worry, I'll wake you up in plenty of time to visit her before the night is out.' Then Tom took up his harp and played a slow, slow air that acted like a lullaby and soon Glasgerion was fast asleep and dreaming of the Lady.

Tom grabbed his coat and made his away to the Lady's hall as fast as he could and when he got there he rattled noisily at the latch. Almost immediately the door opened and the Lady grabbed Tom in her arms and urgently, without waiting to reach the bed, they made love, violently, passionately, there and then, on the floor, just inside the door.

When they had finished and were lying recovering, the Lady remarked that Glasgerion's coat was very rough and that his stockings were holed. Tom, still pretending to be Glasgerion, apologised and said that he had caught his stockings on a briar as he rushed to be with the Lady and, for the same reason, he had grabbed the wrong coat as he left his room. The one he had worn belonged to his little foot page, Tom.

As soon as he could and before his trick was discovered, Tom made good his escape, promising the Lady that he would visit her again, soon, and said that it was the best night he had ever spent, and so on … When he got back to Glasgerion's room he picked up the harp and played a lively, saucy song about lovers being tricked. Glasgerion woke and Tom urged him on.

'Master,' he said. 'The Lady will be waiting for you. While you lay there snoring the finest cock in the land has already crowed!'

Glasgerion rushed as fast as he could to the Lady's hall and rattled and banged on the door. 'Let me in, let me in.'

'It's lovely to see you again but why have you returned so quickly?' she asked. 'Was I not enough for you the first time? I can't believe I left you wanting more. Or did you leave behind a golden ring or have you lost your velvet glove? No, it must be that you cannot wait to sample some more of my love!'

Glasgerion was puzzled and angry. 'Lady, I have never been in this room before,' he shouted. 'I swear it, by oak and ash and bitter thorn. I did not come here tonight.'

'Then who was it that I lay with a few short hours ago?' she wondered. She described how he had come and that his stockings were holey and his coat rough and they realised the trick that Tom had played.

'Woe is me that such a ruffian should lay with me. Never shall the seed of such a rogue grow in my body,' she cried and drew a knife and plunged it into her heart.

Glasgerion stormed home and confronted Tom. 'If I had killed a man tonight,' he said, 'I would tell you. But you have killed three and you don't even know it yet!'

And Glasgerion swept his page's head from his body with his sword. Then he put the point of it against his heart and its pummel on the stone floor and threw himself on it.

And so ends the story of Glasgerion, a warning to all wandering minstrels!

… but, actually the story doesn't end. Glasgerion is alive and well but living under a new identity!

The story of Glasgerion comes from a ballad found in Percy's *Reliques* of 1765. It was then included in Professor Francis James Child's famous collection *The English and Scottish Popular Ballads* in the 1880s (Child #67). Whether the ballad was ever sung we don't know, no tune survives. In 1380 Geoffrey Chaucer wrote of Glasgerion in his book *The House of Fame*, as Bret Glascurion, and he placed him in the musician's gallery alongside other famous musicians such as Orpheus.

In the 1960s, when the British folk revival was under way, A.L. Lloyd, a famous singer, collector and arranger of songs, worked his magic on the ballad and released it to the world as 'Jack Orion'. I had always assumed that it was very much a Bert Lloyd composition based on just a fragment from the past but when you compare his work with Child's Glasgerion, Lloyd actually added or subtracted very little other than changing the name of the main character.

Bert was very generous with his songs and passed them out to anyone whom he thought would benefit from having them and do them justice. Thus, in the 1960/70s 'Jack Orion' was recorded by singers like Bert Jansch, Martin Carthy and Fairport Convention, as well as by Bert Lloyd himself, of course, with Dave Swarbrick on the fiddle.

I had been aware of 'Jack Orion' for a long time through those recordings but only learned it in 1995 to play with our Anglo-Romanian band Popeluc. I felt that the story fitted as well into the life of a Transylvanian fiddle player as it did into a British one. It was made even better when we discovered that we could play 'Jack Orion' and use the Romanian dance tune 'Barbatesc din Sapinta' (men's dance from Sapinta) as a sort of counter-melody! They fitted together perfectly. Perhaps this is not surprising as the tune we have for 'Jack Orion' was made by Bert Lloyd and he was a great fan of Balkan music having done some important collecting in the region. I have very fond memories of playing it in both Maramures and a medieval hall house at the Weald and Downland Open Air Museum in Sussex! It's on our CD *Blue Dor*.

It has been claimed that the character Glasgerion is based on Bardd Glas Geraint (Geraint, the Blue Bard) who lived in Wales in the eighth century CE but there is no proof I can find for this and it is likely to be a back projection by Iolo Morganwg the 'influential Welsh antiquarian, poet and literary forger', to quote Wikipedia.

JACK ORION

Jack Orion he was as good fiddler
As ever fiddled on a string
And he could drive young women wild
With the songs his strings would sing

He could charm the fish out of the sea
Or water out of a marble stone
Or milk out of a young maid's breast
That never with a man had been.

Jack Orion he sat in the castle hall
And he fiddled and he sang 'til they were all asleep
Except that is for the young Lady
And she was wide awake:

And first he played a slow, slow air
And then he played it brisk and gay
And then, dear lord, behind her hand
The Lady she did say

E'er the day is dawned and the cocks have crowed
And flapped their wings so wide
Then you must come to my own bower door
And lay down by my side.

Then Jack wrapped his fiddle in a cloth of green
And he tipped and he toe-ed it out of the hall
And he's gone back home to his page boy Tom
As fast as he can go.

E'er the day is dawned and the cocks have crowed
And flapped their wings so wide
Then I must go to the Lady's bower
And lay down by her side.

Lay down, lay down, my good master
And here's a pillow for your head
I'll wake you up in a very good time
To go to the Lady's bed,

And Tom took the fiddle into his hand
And he fiddled and he sang for at least an hour
And he played his master fast asleep
Then he's off to the Lady's bower

And he didn't take that Lady gay
To blanket or to bed
But right down there on the bedroom floor
He gained her maidenhead!

Then Tom took the fiddle into his hand
And he fiddled and he played a saucy song
Then he's off back home to his dear master
As fast as he can run

Rise up, rise up my dear master
For while you sleep and snore so loud
The finest cock in all the land
Has flapped his wings and crowed.

When Jack Orion came to the door
He twist and he twirled at the pin
Rise up, rise up my own true love
Rise up and let me in.

Did you leave behind a diamond ring
Or did you leave a velvet glove?
Or have you returned back again
To gain some more of my love?

Jack Orion he swore a bloody oath
By oak and ash and bitter thorn
Saying I was never in this room
Since the day that I was born

Well then it was your little foot page
That hath me so beguiled
And woe if such a ruffian
Has given to me a child.

Jack Orion then he went home
Saying Tom, O Tom come here to me
And he hanged the boy from his own gate post
As high as a willow tree.

Pete Castle's rewrite of Bert Lloyd's rewrite of 'Jack Orion' as played by Popeluc and more recently by Pete solo. Popeluc, which existed sporadically from 1995–2005 was Pete Castle: guitar, vocals and doba (drum); Lucy Castle (Pete's daughter): cetera (fiddle), viola; Ioan Pop: zongora (like an adapted guitar), cetera, braci (viola) and vocals. They got together originally to do a one-off short tour, which eventually stretched to about three months and was followed by several other tours all over Britain and occasional work in Romania.

THE DEVIL'S VIOLIN

Many of the stories Glasgerion told have probably been forgotten, as his own story almost was, and so we occasionally need to add some new ones to the canon.

As an introduction to Popeluc performances, I often used to tell the Transylvanian Gypsy story of 'The Devil's Violin', which explains how the Transylvanian Gypsies came to play the violin as their main instrument and why a lot of music from the region, from most of the Balkans in fact, while sounding superficially lively and jolly, has an underlying sense of melancholy.

So we exchange 'Jack Orion' into the Romanian tradition with 'The Devil's Violin' into the British one! It is another story (like 'Binnorie') of using body parts to make a musical instrument.

Somewhere in the forests of northern Romania there was a peasant family – father, mother, a daughter and four sons. Like most people in the area, they had their house and little strip of land on which they grew maize, beans, gourds and peppers; they kept a cow, which they milked, a few hens, and a pony to pull the cart, which the father used for his work collecting wood in the forest and selling it in the nearby towns.

It was a poor life but a happy one.

One morning the daughter, who was just becoming a young woman, was standing outside her father's house when a gentleman rode by on a horse. She called out to him, 'Good morning,' but he didn't show any sign of having heard her, he just rode on. But then the gentry are like that!

Everyone had always told her that she had a beautiful singing voice so the next morning there she was wearing her best dress, with her hair braided, leaning on the wall in what she hoped was a seductive pose and singing as sweetly as she could. When he came by she again called out, 'Good morning, Sir. Isn't it a beautiful day …' But he didn't slow and he didn't answer her … in fact he made no sign of having even seen her.

By now she had decided that she was going to win. She was going to catch that young man and make him her husband, whatever it took. So she turned to the dark arts.

The third morning, as he came riding along, she was standing in the middle of the track holding up a mirror in front of her. She knew that if he looked in the mirror he would be caught, he would be hers, but he obviously knew of this superstition too because, when he saw her standing there he put his arm over his eyes and galloped past without looking.

Deeper, darker spells were needed. The people in that country know a lot about spells and magic and rituals, so she knew what to do.

She took the mirror and placed it in the fork of a tree and she lit a fire that reflected in the mirror and then started performing the necessary rites. I don't know what they were but they went on for most of the night. Words were chanted, notes were sung, steps were danced and various rare herbs were thrown into the flames. After a while, the mirror began to glow and a form took shape within it. A voice spoke: 'If you want me to help you catch that young man then you must give me your mother, your father and your four brothers.'

'Take them,' she cried eagerly, 'anything in return for that young man.' She watched in the mirror as the devil – for it was him – turned her mother, who was a large, shapely woman, into a sort of figure-of-eight-shaped box. Her father, who was tall and thin, became a bow. Her four brothers, who were all different shapes and sizes, became four strings, which he stretched across the box. Then the devil ran the bow across the strings and violin music was heard in the world for the first time.

The next morning, the young woman was standing in her usual place, this time playing the fiddle. Along came the young man, not galloping heedlessly along, but slowly as if being drawn by a string, which he was – the string of the melody she played. When he reached her, he dismounted and they went indoors together and lived together for a year and a day. At the end of that time the mirror that was on the wall over the fireplace began to glow, a voice spoke, and the couple took hands and disappeared into the mirror and were never seen again.

The house gradually fell into ruin and the forest reclaimed it. A tree fell on it and brambles grew out of the roof. Within a few years it was impossible to tell that there had ever been a house there.

More years passed and then, with a huge storm raging, a Gypsy came making his way through the forest. He was tired and wet, so when he saw a mound that would provide a little shelter he tucked himself down behind it. In the morning, when the wind and rain had eased a little, he felt around the mound and discovered a hole like a cave, which made an even better shelter. He forced his way in through the debris and plants and found himself in the ruins of a house. It was an ideal shelter and he thought he'd stay there for a day or two. When it was full daylight, he was able to look around. It had obviously been a nice little house once but it looked as though it had been abandoned with no notice – plates and cups were still on the table and the bed covers, now rotted and mouldy, were pulled back as though someone had just woken up. On a shelf he found a strange figure-of-eight-shaped wooden box with strings on it. He took it down, blew the dust off, and discovered that if he drew the bow, which was lying beside it, across the strings it made a strange, haunting sort of music.

When he resumed his journey he took it with him and over the coming weeks he learned to play it properly and his friends saw it and copied it and soon many of the Gypsies in the area had an instrument like it.

Among themselves the Gypsies probably called it by another name but the local Romanians called it a cetera and the dances they played were hora. The music of the cetera mixed with their favourite drink, which they nicknamed horinca, because it made you want to dance, made for a great time of great emotion – both gaiety and sadness.

And that is why the fiddle became the main instrument of the Gypsies of Transylvania and why their music has that mix of contrasting emotions they call 'dor'.

My tale's ended
T' door sneck's bended;
I went into t' garden
To get a bit of thyme;
I've telled my tale
Thee tell thine.

From South Yorkshire.

AFTERWORD

Into the Twenty-First Century

The stories in this collection form a continuum covering possibly two thousand years or more but the tradition does not suddenly stop; There is no cut-off date for traditional stories, they are always being made. We can't say those made before a particular, random, date can be included here but those afterwards can't. Travelling entertainers have always met with the same kind of adventures – the details change as the world around them changes but the interior truth, the feelings, the interactions with other people, remain the same.

There are several stories included earlier on that seem to have been invented, or perhaps reinvented, within our lifetimes.

I have spent the last forty years travelling the country performing songs and stories in the same way that many of the characters in the stories have. There are a lot of others who have done similarly – storytellers, folk singers, entertainers of many kinds … Alright, I haven't been abducted by fairies or become lost in an enchanted forest, I haven't met and offended a fairy queen or a wizard but I have had adventures that have the same emotional reaction. Some of these incidents I have used as the basis for stories, or have included within other stories that

I tell regularly. Here are a few little anecdotes that could become folk tales in the future.

I usually drive to gigs, mainly because public transport is not very good and even if you can get there it's often difficult to get home again because buses or trains stop running quite early in the evening. It is also difficult to carry your gear – a guitar, a box of CDs, books for sale, plus your clothes and washing stuff on a bus!

Satnavs have made it easier to find your way in broad-brush terms but it can still be difficult to get right to the door, so you occasionally have to ask for help. Experience teaches you that there are some people it is wisest not to ask for directions and others who might be more trustworthy.

Elderly people will probably know where you want to be (unless the name has changed) but they may not know how to direct you there round the new one-way system and no entries. Teenagers will probably send you the wrong way deliberately! Just for a laugh. You'd think a delivery man or courier might be a good bet but very often they come from miles away, have no local knowl- edge, and just follow their own satnavs.

On the occa- sion I am thinking of, I knew I was very close to the venue I was looking for but after driving round for a while I couldn't find it. I reached a crossroads and there, sitting on a bench, was an elderly man. I stopped to ask him if he knew where it was. 'Oh yes,' he said, 'you're not far away, but it's difficult to find. The best thing to do is if I jump in and show you.' So he did. It was complicated. Right here, next left, left again … It would have been very difficult to remember instructions. Then he suddenly said, 'Drop me here, take the next left and you'll see it.' I thanked him and he jumped out of the car and disappeared. It was only as I drove off that I realised I was at the same crossroads that I'd picked him up from!

If I'd been in Ireland I would have thought him to be a leprechaun, in Cornwall he could have been a mischievous pixie but I was not far from Derby.

Accommodation has always been something to think about and must have always been. Back in the days of Glasgerion, minstrels must have had the same problem and come to a deal so that they could sleep in the stable or something similar.

When I first went professional I was doing mainly folk clubs and the custom was for accommodation to be included as part of the deal – otherwise you might need to charge more. It was usually with the club organiser or one of the other regulars. You got the spare bed, or the sofa in the sitting room or, occasionally, just a sleeping bag on the floor, but they were usually very friendly and put themselves out for you. In that way I met some brilliant people and stayed with some of them many times. They became friends.

One drawback was that, sometimes, a crowd of other people would come back as well, they'd bring out the whisky and the singing would start all over again. You'd done your bit and wanted to go to bed but they, your audience, your fans, wanted to hear more.

It wasn't always staying with the organiser, of course. Sometimes they'd book you into a B&B or a simple hotel. On one occasion this turned out to be not much more than a shelter for homeless people and I didn't bother to stay for breakfast!

Storyteller's accommodation is usually of a higher class! Often very cosy B&Bs and on one occasion a top-class hotel where they greeted me with a free glass of wine when I booked in! I haven't had that treatment very often.

Here is the story of a rather uncomfortable night …

I did a gig in a large old building that had been converted into a folk centre. I'd been there several times before and usually stayed in someone's house but this time – probably because the usual accommodation providers were away – they arranged for me to stay in the building. No problem – it had dressing rooms behind the stage with washbasins and toilets and there was a camp bed. It should have been very convenient. I did the gig, which went well. Afterwards I sat in the bar with the organiser while they cleared up and then everyone gradually drifted off home. The organiser showed me my room, made sure I had everything I needed, shook hands and walked off. His last words were, 'Say hello to the ghost for me!'

I don't believe in ghosts. There's no such thing as ghosts. Even if there are they can't hurt you because they have no physical substance. I lay there with these thoughts going through my mind. Any large old building is full of creaks and scratches. Things suddenly go bump in the night for no reason and you are never far from a rat. 'I don't believe in ghosts. There's no such thing as ghosts. Even if there are they can't hurt you because they have no physical substance.' I kept telling myself this over and over, but I could not get to sleep. It must have been about four in the morning before I finally went into a proper sleep.

And then my bedroom door opened and there was a clanking of chains and a shuffling of feet and I leapt awake. I don't think I screamed but I could easily have done. I don't believe in ghosts but who or what had opened my door and come into my room?

It was the cleaner with her mops and buckets. No one had told her I would be there.

Several of the minstrels or fiddlers in these stories had adventures on their way home when they met bulls or fairies or other perils. The way home can be dangerous. You start off full of adrenaline and high from the performance. You perhaps don't take enough care of where you are going and then things go wrong. (On one occasion I drove for miles before I realised I was on the right road but going the wrong way, north instead of south!) When the adrenaline wears off you feel tired and then it gets dangerous.

Driving back down the M1 at about one o'clock in the morning, I became aware of a strange noise, a sort of buzzing, and something in my brain told me that all the while I could hear this buzzing I was alright.

After what seemed an age, but must have been only seconds, I woke up to find myself doing 90mph down the hard shoulder! The buzzing was my off side wheels (driver's side) on the rumble strip between the hard shoulder and the motorway. My feeling was right, all the while I could hear that rumble I was comparatively safe but, if it stopped, it meant I had veered off and was either going across the motorway or down the embankment. In my sleep I must have been steering to keep my wheels on that strip. That woke me up!

From then on I was not so gung-ho about driving home after a gig, I asked for accommodation more often. If I had been a religious person I could say it was my Guardian Angel. If I was superstitious I could thank some lucky spirit or other. I'm not either, so I thank my subconscious mind.

BIBLIOGRAPHY

The stories in this collection have come from a myriad different sources – books, magazines, websites – even word of mouth. Many of them are correlated from different versions. The list below contains major sources that are worth following up. Some of them are available as free downloads. A good source is sacred-texts.com. The best source of all though, and one I deliberately ignored, is The History Press' series of folk tale books.

Addy, Sidney Oldall, *Household Tales & Traditional Remains, Collected in the Counties of York, Lincoln, Derby & Nottingham,* (David Nutt, 1895). It seems impossible to get hold of a copy of the book but it can be found online at www.archive.org/stream/householdtaleswi00addyrich#page/n9/mode/2up

Bottrell, William, *Stories and Folklore of West Cornwall,* 1880.

Briggs, Katherine M. and Tongue, Ruth L. (eds), *Folktales of England,* Routledge & Kegan Paul, 1965.

Bronson, Bertrand Harris, *The Singing Tradition of Child's Popular Ballads,* Princeton University Press, 1976.

Child, Francis James, *The English and Scottish Popular Ballads,* 1888.

Garner, Alan, *Collected Folk Tales,* Harper Collins, 2011.

Hazlitt, W. Carew, *Tales & Legends of National Origin or Widely Current in England from Early Times,* 1899.

Jacobs, Joseph, *English Fairy Tales,* 1890, and *More English Fairy Tales,* 1894, available in several editions, particularly ABC-Clio, 2002 and online.

Jewitt, Llewellyn, *The Ballads and Songs of Derbyshire*, Bemrose & Sons, Derby, 1867.

Keding, Dan and Douglas, Amy (eds), *English Folk Tales*, Libraries Unlimited (Westport, USA), 2005.

MacManus, Seumas, *Donegal Fairy Stories*, McClure Phillips & Co., 1900.

Percy, Bishop Thomas, *Percys Reliques (Reliques of Ancient English Poetry)*, 1765.

Pullman, Philip, *Daemon Voices: essays on storytelling*, David Fickling Books, 2017.

Thomas, W. Jenkyn, *The Welsh Fairy Book*, 1908.

A great source for all kinds of story collections can be found at: sacred-texts.com

A brilliant picture of the life and work of one of the last bards in medieval Britain can be found in Hugh Lupton's novel *The Assembly of the Severed Head*. It's also a very good read:

Lupton, Hugh, *The Assembly of the Severed Head*, Propolis, 2018.

ABOUT THE AUTHOR

'A storyteller who sings half his stories.'
'Using the tradition as a springboard not a straightjacket.'

Two quotes about folk singer and storyteller Pete Castle who has taken his songs and stories up and down the length and breadth of the country (and occasionally abroad) for over forty years, working with both adults and children in just about every sort of setting imaginable (and some that aren't!).

Pete started playing guitar in teenage 'beat groups' in the mid-1960s, found folk music when he went to college, played at being a teacher for a few years and then went professional as a folk singer in 1978. Soon after that, he encountered storytelling and combined the two art forms from then on. The subject matter of this book is therefore ideal for him.

Alongside his performing, Pete has also run a folk show on local radio, appeared several times on TV, written for magazines, lectured and taught for organisations like WEA and Workers Music Association Summer School and, since 1999, been editor of *Facts and Fiction* story-telling magazine.

He had never considered himself a writer until he was asked to write *Derbyshire Folk Tales* for The History Press in 2010. Since then he has produced two more books and written chapters or articles for several more. He would love to be able to show them to his A-level English teacher, who made his life a misery but gave him the kick up the backside he needed!

BY THE SAME AUTHOR

Derbyshire Folk Tales (The History Press, 2010).

Nottinghamshire Folk Tales (The History Press, 2012).

Where Dragons Soar and other Animal Folk Tales of the British Isles (The History Press, 2016).

Nine Witch Locks – A Retelling of the Ballad Willie's Lady in Ballad Tales (The History Press, 2017).

'My Journey Into Storytelling', a chapter in *An Introduction to Storytelling* (The History Press, 2018).

Over the years Pete has also recorded a couple of dozen albums on cassette, LP and CD. Those still available are:

Poor Old Horse
The Outlandish Knight
Mearcstapa
False Waters
Tapping at the Blind (stories)
Blue Dor (with Popeluc)
The Derby Ram (songs from Derbyshire; various artists)
Oyster Girls & Hovelling Boys (songs from Kent; various artists)

For more info or to purchase, see Pete's website (which is also the *Facts and Fiction* website) https://petecastle.co.uk